Chastity BLACK

UNDERCOVER AGENT FOR THE BRITISH SECRET SERVICE

TAY LAWRENCE

Copyright

All rights reserved. Chastity Black by Tay Lawrence, in its current format, copyright © Tay Lawrence 2015. Cover Illustration Copyright © 2015 by Clockwork Content Publishing

This book in part or in whole, may not be copied or reproduced in its current format by any means, digital, in print or otherwise without written permission, except for quotations for review purposes only.

Clockwork Content
10 Shakespeare House,
37-39 Shakespeare Street,
Southport
Merseyside.
PR8 5AB
www.clockworkcontent.com
email: press@clockworkcontent.com
ISBN-13: 978-1508761181
ISBN-10: 1508761183

Disclaimer

This is a work of fiction. Names, characters, businesses, places, events and incidents are the product of the author's imagination and used in a fictitious manner. Any resemblance to actual persons, agencies or organisations living or dead, or actual events is purely coincidental.

For Joe. You know why.

UNDERCOVER AGENT FOR THE BRITISH SECRET SERVICE

Prologue

Constance slid further behind the bar. She could hear the familiar footsteps on the deck getting closer. She stifled the scream that was threatening. She needed to control herself or she would give herself away. Bringing her hand up to her sore cheekbone, she winced as she touched it. No question it was broken by the power of the blows that had rained down on her.

Wiping her mascara streaked eyes, she held her breath as she heard the door to the room groan as it opened. Trying to make herself smaller, Constance strained to hear where her attacker was. What a fool she had been. She thought it was just going to be an average date on a luxury yacht, how mistaken could she be?

If she got out of this, she was going to change her ways. No more escort work.

Listening to the footsteps receding back on deck, Constance let out a breath. There was a small motor boat tied to the back of the yacht, *or was it called the stern? What was she thinking? Did it matter what the frigging thing was called,* she thought? *She was about to be murdered?*

She waited a few minutes, raising her head above the mahogany bar. The room was dark, but she could just make out the soft lighting on deck beyond the glass doors. The boat was steady and the motor was silent. They were still. She had no idea how far from land they were. Under the blanket of the night sky there was no way of knowing what direction she was going in. But what other choice did she have?

If she could swim to the motorboat she just might have a chance. *Didn't they have radios on those things?* She stood, willing her legs to move. Her bare feet were bleeding from the broken glass in the cabin during the struggle.

With caution she edged out from behind the bar and tip-toed towards the doors ever watchful. With as much care as possible,

Constance pulled the door towards her, flinching at the squeak it made.

The deck was silent. Her feet raged with pain as she limped towards the back of the boat. Almost crying with relief, she saw it - the boat bobbing on the water behind the yacht. Stealing up to it wary of the voices she heard somewhere below; she began tying off the rope that attached the boat to the yacht. Working in haste at the knot she sighed, rewarded with the slack hope that she was going to make it.

Then she heard it - the heavy breathing behind her. As she turned in fear, her world was turning black; the last thing she would see was the hammer as it came down on her like thunder.

Chapter One

I picked up the glass, sipping the water. Had I completely lost my mind? Not only was I risking my job at MI5, there was a chance I could get locked up for working the field on a personal basis without authorization. *Jesus, what would the Head of Security think if he found out?*

I fiddled with my robe. It felt soft on my skin as I looked around at the other girls waiting with me at the hotel suite. We were all naked under our towelling gowns. What were we expected to do when we entered the other room?

The large wooden door swung open, and another girl came out of the interview room. Her face flushed as she caught my eye and gave me a nervous glance. I looked up at the woman standing by the door. She was a mousy little thing with that look that rabbits get when they're caught in the headlights of an oncoming truck.

"Please," she said while ushering me through with a flourish of her hand. "I believe your next."

It was clear that this was not the head honcho. This woman was way too nervous and harried looking to be able to be the head of the classiest escort agency in the Country. I gave a thin smile as I stepped past her, the scent of lavender hung off her like an old lady's handbag.

"Good afternoon. It's Ms Blake, I believe?"

The elegant, well dressed woman sitting on the plush sofa looked at her notes. She was completely different to her dowdy assistant. She was in her late thirties, attractive with shoulder length brown hair. Golden highlights accented her warm skin tone. Everything about her screamed high maintenance and expensive living.

"Yes," I lied. "Carla Blake"

"My name is Cordelia Bainbridge. This is my assistant, Miss Childers. Please ignore my colleague behind me. He is here only for security reasons."

I hadn't noticed the well built man sitting on a chair by the window. What was he? A bodyguard of some kind? With his brown hair and the brown suit he was wearing he blended into the chocolate walls of the room like a chameleon. He showed no interest anyway. He had no doubt seen this a thousand times before, like a chef, who's fed up with the sight of food when he gets home from work.

"Now please take your robe off," said Cordelia Bainbridge. Her perfect clipped English accent sounded shrill to my ears.

This was more like it. Now this is the head honcho. Classy, attractive and assertive. Her words imply an order, not a request. Normally I'd insist on being bought a drink first before I strip. Hell, how about a meal to go with that drink? Obeying the demand, I untied the belt of the robe letting it fall by my feet. I remembered I was doing this for Connie. Without a shred of shame I stood rooted, revealing all my nakedness to three perfect strangers.

"Hmm," she murmured, as she stood and walked towards me, her brows knitted as she inspected me at close quarters. With perfect confidence she reached out a hand and extending her long, slim fingers stroked my pussy. "I see you wax. Good. Our clients like their dates shaved. As they are the wealthiest and most powerful in the world they expect only the best."

Yeah, sure. Whatever. Am I for real? Am I applying for a job to be a billionaire plaything? Me, Chastity Black, an escort? I wanted to punch this woman square in the face and I'm pretty sure I could knock her brown suited gorilla into next week if need be.

She touched me again allowing her fingers to linger on my pussy. I was quite certain she did not need to. After all, we had already ascertained I'm a shaven Raver. But as her fingers stroked my velvet folds, I started to tingle. This woman knew what she was doing. With a quiet confidence she looked me in the eye and smiled.

"You're perfect. Tall, blond, curvy but athletic and you have such beautiful breasts." Her manicured fingers stroked them tracing a light touch around my nipple following the contour of their roundness.

If my mother could see me, she'd be turning in her grave. All that convent education for Connie and I to end up like this. My stomach flipped at the thought of Connie. No, Connie didn't end up like this. Connie was dead, perhaps because of this. I would never forget the moment I saw her at the hospital morgue for as long as I lived. Her broken and beaten body discarded like an old bag of rubbish thrown into the Thames only to wash up the following day.

Bainbridge must have noticed me stiffen and edged back to her sofa to look at her notes.

"Well, Ms Blake," she began as she glanced back at her file. "I see you're 24. That's good. We have a strict cut off policy of 27. But if you do well, in the next two years you should have secured a tidy sum of money if you invest it with a little savvy. You could make quite a few million. I can tell you will be much in demand by our clients."

Yeah 24, honest. Maybe four years ago. Feigning a thankful smile, I nod in agreement.

"Providing you pass the background checks and the medical we'll schedule for you, I think we can start you next week."

Lucky for me, I'm skilled in suppressing my emotional responses. My chest tightened at the idea of the background check. Hugo had not yet agreed to provide me with the cover and the backstory I asked for. He wasn't forthcoming when I spoke to him. I prayed he had not told the Assistant or Head of Security at MI5 what I'm up to; otherwise I'm on my way to a nice cell. Do not pass go or collect £200. Go straight to jail.

Another thought hit me. If Hugo did not back up my cover with the escort agency, whoever killed Connie would be onto me. I picked up my robe aware of the danger and the risks. Fuck it. To hell with the consequences. It was the only way to find out why my sister was killed and what was more important, who did it.

Chapter Two

There was no time to lose. I pulled up, parking my Audi in Hugo's driveway. It had taken me almost one and half-hours to drive to his house in Oxford. Traffic was murder. I pulled out the pay-as-you go phone I'd purchased the day before. It was the one with the number I'd given the agency for Hugo. So far, so good. They had not tried calling him yet. I still had time to persuade him.

I'd always liked Hugo Fitzcharles. I'd known him since I had joined '5' three years earlier, and he had become one of my closest friends. He had a way about him that made me feel safe and he had always been able to make me laugh, no matter what the circumstances. If I could have chosen a father for myself and Connie, Hugo would be it. Although his sexual preference for young men would have made that quite impossible. With his greying hair and British mannerism, he was every inch the silver fox.

I was rewarded with his scowl as soon as I rang his doorbell.

"I don't need MI5 or Special Branch to tell me why you're here, do I," said Hugo standing on his front porch? He looked quaint and dapper in his black slacks, a v-neck yellow sweater and carpet slippers.

"Just let me talk to you please Hugo? This is important."

"You'd better come in then. Can't imagine what anyone would say finding a ravishing young girl on my doorstep. I'd lose my credibility with all those attractive young men."

Once inside, Hugo guided me through to his lounge. I had always loved his house. It had a smell of furniture polish along with the chimes from his old grandfather clock in the hallway. It reminded me of our first home as children before our father left and everything turned to shit.

"I need that cover story," I blurted out, "and a safe house I can use as a front. You know I'm going through with it, with or without your help? But with would be better."

"You know what you're asking me?"

"I would not ask at all if I didn't need you. But for chrissake Hugo, my sister was murdered and it's my fault. I have to find out why she was killed and who killed her. It's my obligation."

"Why on earth would you feel obligated? You didn't even get on with your sister. You told me you could not stand her."

"I know. It's not that." I felt like sinking into Hugo's thick red Chinese rug, letting it swallow me up. I winced at the thought of the complaints I had made about my sister. I hated myself for it now. After all, I would never get to complain about her again. "She called me the night she died and I didn't answer."

Hugo folded his arms. He nodded at me to continue.

"I figured it would be another of her dramas, another man problem. She was always getting in with the wrong crowd and I was fed up bailing her out all the time. So just this once I thought I'd make her clean up her own mess. And because of that, she's dead." Since discovering her death only three days earlier, the guilt had been close to choking me. It felt a relief to tell someone.

"You don't know that Chastity. Her calling you could have had nothing to do with her death. It's a police matter, not one for MI5."

"Oh come on Hugo, the police just see it as an everyday druggy prostitute gets killed scenario."

"Why would they think that? Constance was a drug user?"

"No way. She had a rare pituitary dysfunction. Even prescribed drugs had little effect on her. But the post mortem showed traces of heroin in her blood stream."

"I'm sorry Chastity. You can see that she was beyond your help then?"

"You don't get it Hugo. There was only one puncture wound in her arm. A real drug user would have track lines everywhere. No, someone made it look like she was on drugs to avoid any suspicion." Scraping my hair off my face, I looked into Hugo's eyes pleading with him.

"What have the police said," Hugo replied averting my gaze? I knew the modus operandi. Answer a question with a question to deflect having to answer the question.

"I've only spoke with them on the phone. They know she was working for an escort agency, but the manager there told them she was not booked out that night, not by them anyway. I don't buy any of it. I have to get to the bottom of it for my sister. I've let her down. When our mother died, I should have kept a tighter hold on Constance, but instead I concentrated on my own career."

"You know you're supposed to be on leave? As Chief of Staff I could get into deep water even helping you. It's completely unsanctioned, not to mention wasting security resources for personal use."

"I'm willing to take the risk. Please Hugo, I'm begging you to provide me with a cover? I have to do this."

"Alright. But if we get found out we're both for the high jump, not to mention a stay at her majesty's pleasure in a secure institution."

Smiling at his words, I could not help feeling relieved. "I'd of thought being surrounded by men vying for your body would appeal to you."

As Hugo walked over to his cabinet pouring us both a scotch and soda, I could see he was still worried about it.

"You know what would be involved going undercover at an escort agency? You'll be expected to have a lot of sex."

"Hugo, I've done it all before, only before I did it for Queen and Country. When I was seconded to MI6 they put me in deep, working on the Tier 2 splinter group. I ended up having sex with three men in a hot tub in Morocco." I took a sip of Scotch. "You should know I'm hardened to such things."

"Yes and if I remember correctly, you ended up shooting them after."

"That was regrettable, yes and unfortunate. But what could I do? They made me when the tracking device fell out of my bag" I tried to stifle the smile. The Moroccan four-way was one of the most erotic and pleasurable nights I'd ever had. Starting with an invitation from one of the group leaders, it was important to gain their trust. It seemed joining them naked in a hot tub was proof of my commitment to their cause. I licked my lips as I savoured the memory. I'd been taken every which way that night by the three Middle Easterners. It lasted for over 3 hours. They were the most attractive targets I'd ever had. And as for their beautiful cocks. I'd never seen such size and experienced such exquisite taste from a dick before. I was drenched in their cum before we'd even finished, not to mention my dripping pussy they couldn't get enough of. Pity I had to shoot them in the end. I'd have enjoyed more over the coming weeks.

Hugo patted me on the shoulder. "Lucky you, at least you got your foursome first. You get all the breaks and the fun."

"So will you give me a cover and keep it secret?"

"OK, but you need to do what you have to do as quick as possible. Sooner or later someone from Thames House will catch on and then we're both sunk. Understand?"

The solemn silence was broken up by the silly James Bond tune that chirped from the pay-as-you-go mobile.

"It's for you," I said, passing Hugo the phone.

"Yes, funny ringtone," he said, shaking his head. "Hilarious even. Why would it be for me?" He cringed at the sound.

"Because I bought a couple of pay as you go phones. This one is yours; I gave the number to the escort agency and told them that's how they could reach you."

Hugo shook his head. The smile that appeared on his wizened face revealed that my humour and barefaced cheek had somewhat tickled him. Pressing the answer key, I watched him with intense scrutiny as he spoke to the caller.

"Yes... yes. She's been with my company for 4-years. Yes, that's right since she was 20."

I listened for a full twenty minutes as Hugo answered question after question about me. Finally he hung up and shot me a curious look.

"Well, that was unusual. So you're Carla Blake, aged 24 eh?"

I rolled my eyes. "Shaving four years off my age is not the worst thing I've done in my life as you well know."

"I think you might be onto something though. They ask more questions than any of the terrorist groups we have infiltrated. They do appear to have some trust issues. But yes, they think I have a computer business, and you have been my assistant. I'll get someone on the team to build the website and set the cover up for you." Hugo opened his battered brown leather briefcase and passed me an envelope. "Here's the keys to an apartment that's been cleared and is a good front.

Taking the envelope, I thanked Hugo before I placed it in my pocket.

"Be careful though Chastity. I told them what you wanted me to, but I'm not sure they believed me. They were more thorough than I would have thought. I just hope your cover has not already been blown."

I didn't need reminding of the risks. But this time I was not going to let down my little sister.

"And if you get into trouble," continued Hugo, "you can't even call for back-up. You'll be completely on your own."

Chapter Three

I woke to the early morning sun streaming through the white curtains. It was my first night at the apartment. And what an apartment. Sometimes safe or cover houses can be a bit drab, but this was pure luxury. Positioned right in the middle of fashionable Kensington, it was so big that my own little poky one bedroom flat could have fitted 6 times in this place.

Of course I could never afford such a property on my own meagre salary. But good old Hugo had come through trumps this time. It fitted in with the cover story I told E agency.

I felt a little safer now that Hugo had backed me up. I had emailed the escort agency the previous night and updated my profile along with my new swanky address.

I sounded like a spoiled little rich kid on my resume. An only child with a wealthy mummy and daddy living it up in Switzerland. Sadly, it was far from the truth. The only scrap of truth being that, yes, there was once a rich daddy, but he left, taking his money with him leaving two children. I had not seen him since I was 8 and Connie 5. As for dear old mum, well, even all her religious vigour didn't save her from a life inside a bottle, usually a Vodka one. Perhaps if she had been able to beat the drink early on, she'd still be alive now.

I enjoyed the feeling of the cool Indian cotton sheets under my skin. As I lay there thinking what I had to do, my thoughts turned to Connie, I awoke from my musings by the ringing of the phone. It was the 5th Symphony ringtone - well mum had always favoured Beethoven. Turning to the bedside table I picked up the mobile. It was the twin handset. The other pay-as-you-go phone I'd bought along with Hugo's and only one number programmed into it - E. Escort Agency.

Pressing the green call button I listened. This was the call I'd been hoping for and dreading at the same time. Had my cover been blown?

"Hello," began the voice at the other end of the line. "Is this Carla?"

I recognized the voice immediately. It was unsure and measured.

"This is Elizabeth Childers. We met yesterday."

"Oh, hello," I said, sounding surprised. I was anything but surprised. But it was a good start. If it was Bainbridge herself, who called me, then I'd known my cover was blown. No, an assistant calling me was more realistic. I was pretty sure I had passed their background checks. God bless Hugo.

"We have booked you an appointment with our private physician at his clinic in Harley Street for 11.10 tomorrow morning Ms Blake."

Bingo - I was in. I needed to gather as much intelligence about the set-up of the escort agency as possible. So far, I'd come up with diddly squat. I didn't even have a real address for E, and even their phone number was registered to a virtual office. I needed to work fast. I was aware that time was most definitely not on my side.

"Is there any chance I could have an earlier appointment," I asked? I could hear papers rustling down the line along with a pause in the conversation.

"I'm afraid not. There are other staff booked in earlier. Why is this time a problem?"

"No, not at all. I'll be there." I said my goodbyes and hung up. I had a whole day to think it all through.

After dragging myself from the sumptuous queen sized bed, I ambled into the large open plan kitchen. It overlooked the street and the park opposite. Pulling the screen down I was blinded for a moment by the sun. As I adjusted my eyes to allow for the light, I caught sight of a black Ford Focus parked opposite and a man sitting at the wheel. I couldn't make out his face; the sun visor was down and hiding his features from view. Maybe nothing, but all the same, it was worth being mindful about it. In my profession, vigilance is paramount.

After showering and dressing I made myself some toast as I ran through what I knew so far. My sister was not a consultant to a travel bureau as she had me believe.

Instead, she was an escort for a high class agency that was selective and secretive. At some time between the 3pm phone call I'd received from Connie that Saturday night and

8am the next morning she had been killed. Her body found washed up in the estuary. The biggest tell was the traces of Heroin. Whoever injected her didn't know about her intolerance to drugs. They wanted to make it look like a drug associated death, perhaps trouble with a dealer.

I took another glance through the blind. Yup, just as I suspected. The Ford Focus was still parked. It looked like surveillance to me. But whose? Was it 5's, and if so, how did they find out so soon? I pulled back my long blond hair, securing it with a rubber band. It was more likely to be the agency watching. But why?

The next morning I arrived at the clinic in Harley Street. Again, this was no cheap affair. Another expensive establishment, paid for by E. Escorts. It made me wonder how powerful these people were.

"Hi, my name is Carla Blake. I have an appointment at 10.30 am." Giving my sweetest smile to the receptionist I threw a quick glance about the room. These places always have the same type of women working on their receptions. Lots of makeup, French polished nails, tailored clothing to go with their tailored voices. There were women like this up and down the breadth of Harley Street. Was there a little factory buried somewhere manufacturing these clones?

"Um... sorry, we have you down for 11.10."

"Oh must be my mistake. I'll just wait then." Scanning the waiting room, I sized up the patients waiting. There were some new girls, just like me. You can tell immediately by their nervous look and fidgeting. One girl, however, looked all too relaxed. Perhaps she was not so new after all. Taking the seat next to her I slyly appraised her. I could tell she was one of E's. Channel bag, Dior dress and Jimmy Choos'.

"Hi, I'm Carla. You with the agency?"

"Yes." She looked at me unsure.

"It's my first time. You?" I already knew she was a seasoned pro, but hey, why not just play along for a while?

"No, I've been with them six months now. I'm just here for my 3-monthly. They like you to have regular blood tests and checks."

"Are they good to work for?"

"It can get a little crazy. It depends if you're game for anything."

"What's your name," I asked her?

"I'm called Skylar. It's not my real name. They give you a new one when you start work."

"So what kind of crazy things do you mean?"

"Well, there are a lot of parties and anything goes. Most of the clients tend to book the girls in twos or threes. So I hope you have an open mind." Skylar looked at me. I could tell by the direction her eyes moved over me, she was trying to suss me out. I must have a trusting face as I could see her relax - sitting back her shoulders slumped against the leather chair. As if in a conspirational move, she edged closer towards me. Anyone watching would think she was divulging state secrets.

"Last weekend I was flown to Paris with Candy, another girl who works for the agency," she said, keeping her voice low. "We partied with a group of European financiers. It got a bit mad. Sometimes I had to deal with five of them at the same time. But I got a ten thousand pound tip for my trouble and you could say I was quite satisfied when I got home.

I bet she was, the saucy trollop. "What are the clients like?"

"Some can be quite good looking. Wealthy of course."

"So why do they have to pay for escorts?" I also knew the answer to this, but I still needed to sound a little naive for appearances sake.

"I think they like to know they can get as freaky as they like without complaint. The tips at the end of the night are always generous the more you do."

"Where do these parties take place?" I tried to sound casual and interested.

"Oh, that can be anywhere, from the most expensive hotels to luxury yachts and villas. You can get to travel a lot with these guys. The perks are fantastic."

Smiling, I picked up a glossy magazine from the polished coffee table. "Does it ever get rough?"

"No. The men do tend to like us to be submissive. But I guess that's to be expected. Of course, there are the clients that get off on being dominated too."

Yeah. No shit. "Sounds OK," I replied. I'm lying through my teeth. Me submissive? Hugo would laugh for a year if he heard me playing along with this. I like my men where I want them - underneath me and completely in my control.

"How many girls are there at the agency?"

"I don't know, to be honest. Faces come and faces go. There's been quite a few."

Nodding, I try to push further without causing suspicion. "Do you have many friends there?"

"I used to, but it's not worth getting too close to anyone in case you never see them again." Skylar smoothed her already perfect brown hair, her face tensing a little around the eyes.

"You mean if they leave?" I tried to reassure her with another winning smile, but I could sense she was starting to feel uncomfortable with my questions.

"I guess so," she continued. "Sometimes they just disappear without a trace like they've vanished from the face of the world. I guess they move on and don't want to be found."

I watched as Skylar perfected her smile again. It was obvious she was trying to regain her composure.

"I don't plan on doing this for too long myself," she continued. "I'm saving most of my money and in a few years I should be able to open my own restaurant in London."

Feeling the hairs on the back of my neck rise, I tried to look relaxed. "Sounds like a great investment." I hoped Skylar would one day get her wish. "I suppose when you want to settle down and have a family or a life, the last thing you want is someone finding out about what you used to do."

Or maybe you vanish because you get killed and your body gets dumped in the Thames?

Chapter Four

All seemed to be going well. I had just had a call from Elizabeth Childers. She'd given me the address of E's headquarters in Chelsea. With the background checks and medical completed, I had somehow been accepted. I looked at the location. It looked swish and up-market. I was expected to arrive the next morning for my induction.

So far, so good. I now had premises. It was time to make headway. Roll on tomorrow.

The house was more than I expected. Cloistered behind an expensive neighbourhood, it was obvious that they administered good security. I drove up to the entrance. Two large wrought iron gates flanked by a massive perimeter wall barred my way. I looked along the top of the red brick fortress. CCTV cameras perched atop every few meters. These people took no chances. I smiled as my window buzzed when I lowered it. I looked up at the camera at the gate and was rewarded with a metallic clang as the gates sprang open allowing me entry. I was never getting into this residence unnoticed, that was for sure. I'd been in foreign consulates that looked like frigging walk in clinics compared to this place.

The drive up to the house wound along roughly half a mile. If I didn't know any better I'd have sworn it was a private hospital. Finally, I came to a circled area surrounded by lawns and a fountain. There were a couple of cars already there, but no Black Ford Focus. Parking my car, I walked up to the door and rang the buzzer. I looked clearly into the camera fixed above the entrance and smiled.

"Welcome. It's nice to see you again."

I wasn't surprised to see Miss Childers sitting behind a large mahogany desk in the foyer. I looked around. "Wow, this place is huge. It's fabulous." I was not lying, it was. From the hallway, a large lush red carpeted stairway led upwards to a gallery. There must have been at least 20 rooms in the place, not counting basements and outbuildings. What on earth went on here?

Miss Childers stood shaking my hand. Her palm felt sweaty and limp.

"You're a little early, but just take a seat. We're waiting on the other girls who are starting with you."

"I was worried I would be late. The roads are so busy this time of a morning, so I left earlier," I lied. My timely arrival was more to do with seek and find and not any concern about traffic. I took the offered seat.

This was an expensive setup. The house was decorated in tasteful hues of green and red. Wooden banisters, doors and floors shone from beeswax with a number of rooms off the main hallway. As I scanned above my head, I became aware of the CCTV camera behind Miss Childers' desk. It was security overkill. What were these people so paranoid about? The house itself was quiet except for the tapping Miss Childers made on her keyboard.

"I'm sorry to interrupt, but can you point me to the bathroom?"

Taking her spectacles off, Miss Childers rubbed her eyes then pointed past me. "The toilet's just through that door, down the steps on the left."

Thanking her with a weak smile I trotted off in my six inch heels in the right direction. I wondered how someone as drab and plain as Elizabeth Childers got to work for an agency like E? It wasn't because of her choice in polyester blouses that was for sure.

I found the loo and carried on past it. At the end of the corridor was another flight of stone steps. As I rounded the corner, I found they carried on down. I paused as I heard hollow voices coming from somewhere below. I took off my Blahnik's, lest their stiletto heel reveal my presence as I tiptoed down the steps. When I almost reached the bottom, I leaned my head from the wall. Below was what must have been the security room. I could make out the bank of monitors on the wall. The place had more eyes than a nest of spiders. Seeing enough, I retreated back the way I'd come.

I'd just got to the top of the stone steps and managed to slip my shoes back on when I was caught off guard. It was the same brown suited gorilla that was present during my interview at the hotel.

"What are you doing?"

Typical for the likes of him. No introduction just information. He looked at me as though he meant business. He had a squat little neck, holding his round head; the tension of his suit straining from the muscles beneath. This bloke needed a break from the steroids or the gym. That much was obvious.

"Oh... sorry. I was looking for the bathroom. It's a big place," I giggled. *Yep, play the dumb blond Chastity. It's what these idiots think about you anyway.*

"The toilet's that way," he grunted as he nodded his head behind him.

No, no sense of humour coming from him any time soon.

"Thanks," I said. I walked past him, then paused as we stood face-to-face. "I don't believe I got your name the other day..."

"That's because I didn't give it."

I remained silent as he eyed me. With one sweep of his eyes over my body, he gave one last contemptible glance down his nose at me then sauntered past. Yep, this man was a real charmer.

The other girls had arrived by the time I got back to the reception area. These were indeed top totty. Three girls adorned the seats in the hallway - two brunettes and another blond. I recognized the blond from the interview at the hotel. They looked at me as I registered their cool appraisal.

I never understood why women were so competitive. But even in '5', there seemed to be an undercurrent of cattiness within the ranks. Men were different. It was all about success, money and power. Any psychologist would have told them it was all to do with insecurity and penis size envy. I mean, why do men have to compete about what car they have and how much they earn? They should all just get their dicks out and slap them on a table - whoever has the biggest wins. It's that simple.

The throaty cough emitted by Miss Childers pulled me from my thoughts.

"Please follow me," she said. "Ms Bainbridge is waiting for you in the boardroom."

What, escorts having a board meeting? What was this? Were we going to be offered a pension plan, have a sex strategy brainstorm session?

The four of us followed the tired looking receptionist along another corridor and then into a grand looking room. An expansive wooden table, taking centre stage with carved wooden chairs accompanying it. On the table were four glasses, Evian water, pens and a clear plastic wallet at each seat. I smoothed my hair, checking everything was in place. I'd opted for a French bun. It had taken me ages perfecting the style.

"Good morning ladies. It's a pleasure to see you all again. Today is your induction. There is coffee on the cabinet behind you, should you wish to pour yourself a cup."

Was this for real? An induction? What was going to be shared with us? *How to have sex part 1, health and safety? All hard hats must be worn on site along with safety glasses?* Then again, I could see how the goggles could come in handy in this line of work.

"There are some points that I need to go over with you," began Bainbridge. "But before I start, I will tell you that you are required to sign a confidentiality agreement today."

It didn't come as a surprise to me. But one of the brunettes, the one with the long curvy legs didn't look too pleased at the news.

"Nothing that is said by either myself or any of the clients is ever to be spoken about," continued Bainbridge. "We are strict on security. But we are dealing with powerful and in some cases, well known clients. So I'm sure you can understand the importance of confidentiality."

Yeah. No shit, Sherlock.

"Of course, because of our excellent confidentiality clauses, we have a great reputation. As a result, our girls are handsomely recompensed." Bainbridge scanned our faces one-by-one, resting on mine a little too long in my opinion.

"What happens if someone breaks the agreement?"

I wondered this myself, but was thankful when Miss long legs with the brown hair had asked it.

"We have the best solicitors," replied Bainbridge addressing the brunette. "Any break in confidentiality or security is dealt with in the most severe way. If any of you have any problem with this, please leave now."

"What about our confidentiality? We don't want anyone knowing what we do either."

As none of the girls had been introduced to each other I was thankful for this inquisitive young lady in her dogged persistence. The more she asked, the less I had to, thus averting suspicion.

"Of course your protection and security are paramount. Each of you will be given a new name here. You will be known by this name to the clients and to each other. It is also forbidden to divulge your real names to clients. To do so, will result in immediate dismissal. But we will get to that later in the one-to-one interview."

Ms Bainbridge's eyes glanced at me. Was that the faintest of smiles I could detect on her face? I watched as she smoothed down her blouse. Her hardened nipples were visible through the sheer cotton. She bit into her lower lip before passing another glance my way.

"Because security is important," she said. "We exercise strict rules that you must adhere to." Bainbridge's face immediately darkened. Whatever she was about to say she was serious about.

"Moonlighting is not allowed. You will not work for any other agency or as an individual while you are in our employ. Also, no boyfriends are permitted. We insist that all girls have no ties. This is another reason why you have been chosen. We do not want emotional and angry boyfriends or partners or parents. Understood?"

It made perfect sense to me. I wondered if this could also be another motive for Connie's murder. I mean what did I know about her personal life? I always pushed her away. No wonder she could never confide in me. I was not surprised my sister kept her escort life to herself. I had not been the most endearing listener to her woes. Maybe there was a boyfriend. Maybe he found out what she did and killed her. There was only line of attack to deal with this, and that was to get to the bottom of it. One way or another.

"Besides," continued Bainbridge. "You should find we keep you busy enough to need to seek elsewhere for a relationship." She paused in her speech before giving a faint smile. "Some of our clients are skilled in the sexual arena, as are the girls here."

"What if the client asks for something I'm not comfortable with?"

It was the brunette again. Even I noticed this girl was asking way too many questions for comfort.

"Then you're in the wrong profession," replied our hostess. "The client's satisfaction is your top priority. The client's needs must always come first."

Not if I can help it. I always like to come first. The man only coming when he has my permission.

"What if the client gets rough?"

Bainbridge took a moment as she eyed this mouthy girl. She had a slight northern accent that was just about discernible. It was though she was trying to hide it. I examined the girl closely. I could spot a pair of Jimmy Choo knock offs anywhere. And her Gucci bag looked the biz, but I could still tell it was another fake.

"It does not happen. Most of our clients are regulars or referred to us on recommendation. They know the rules. On your first assignment, you will be accompanied by another member of staff anyway." Ms Bainbridge picked up a plastic wallet. "All the information you need is in here. And as a way of introducing you to some of our clients, a party has been arranged this Saturday night. Your presence is compulsory. But trust me, it will be enjoyable."

I didn't doubt that it could be. But having to have sex with someone regardless of whether you want to or not was not my thing. Although I had done it before on numerous occasions as an operative in the field. There wasn't a lot of difference, except of course this way paid well more than I earned in the Security Service.

As though she was reading my mind. Bainbridge carried on.

"You earn a monthly retainer of £10,000, plus your fee for any appointment. This is in the region of "£5,000 and £20,000 depending on length of time and venue. And then of course there are your tips, which as any of the other girls will testify are generous. You are also allowed to accept gifts from clients."

I looked at the other two girls faces. They looked quite happy, but I didn't think Miss Legs looked satisfied as she ran her hand through her long brown hair.

Standing up, Bainbridge addressed us. "Right I think we have covered everything. Now if you would like to sit in reception. I'll call you on an individual basis into my office for contract signing and name assignment."

Chapter Five

When we returned to the reception area, I noticed that Bainbridge's security guard was milling around. His ever watchful gaze focused on us. Not being able to take advantage of the time to snoop, I had no option but to wait with the others. I drank coffee while Bainbridge buzzed Childers to send each of us in one by one. It was no surprise that she left me to last.

"It's good to see you here Carla. I'd hoped you would return."

"Thank you Ms Bainbridge." I allowed my eyes to rest on hers for a moment longer than necessary. She didn't break from my gaze. This woman was steel through and through. It was difficult to see through her facade. I was good at reading people, but Cordelia Bainbridge was tough.

Bainbridge arranged the sheets of paper on her desk. "First, I chose the name Mercedes for you."

"Sounds good." I replied. "Why Mercedes?"

Passing me a wad of papers, she licked her lips then smiled. "I have always found them to be beautiful cars. I drive one myself. I love the feel of the interior and the smell of the leather. They are exquisite machines."

Nodding at this, I would not be thanking her for her compliment. I did not appreciate being compared to a piece of machinery. Something about this woman sent cold waves all the way down my spine. Taking the pen she offered me, I signed away all rights to my freedom on the dotted line. Instead, I exchanged handsome compensation for my silence. God, it was like working for MI5 all over again.

As I handed the papers back to Bainbridge, the rapping on the door pulled her attention from me.

"Yes," she called. I could not mistake the annoyance in her voice.

I turned to see who it was. I know I was being nosy, but hey, that's what I was there for. Miss Childers stood at the threshold looking more nervous than usual. Her fingers tapping her knuckles.

"Yes, Miss Childers. I told you I didn't want to be disturbed," said Bainbridge.

"There is errm... someone here to see you. He said it was important."

Bainbridge raised a shaped eyebrow. "That's fine. Tell our visitor I'll be along in a moment." She turned her attention back to me. "If you could wait a moment, I won't be too long."

It was clear she had not finished with me yet. I'd been getting overt sexual signals from her since I'd entered the room. Did she have the hots for me or something? If it was any other place of work, she'd be asking to be sued for sexual harassment. But I doubt in an escort agency, something like that would stand.

I listened as I heard her footsteps recede. Wasting no time, I went straight to the filing cabinet behind her desk. This was my only chance, and I had no idea how long Bainbridge would be. Reaching a hand into my elaborate French bun, my fingers found what I had been looking for. I pulled out the two long metal picks from my hair and placed them in the lock on the cabinet. Within moments I heard the familiar click. There wasn't a locked door or cabinet I could not get into. I was famous for it at '5'.

With a whistle, I thanked God. I found what I was looking for in the top drawer. She was filed under her real name 'Constance Black'. I pulled the file with deft fingers from the drawer and laid them out on Bainbridge's desk. I didn't have enough time to read them, so taking my mobile phone from my pocket, I found the app I was looking for and pressed. The camera snapped away. I had just scanned the last sheet when I heard voices. Without wasting a moment I put everything back and closed the drawer just in time to move to the window.

The door opened. I stood rooted looking out onto the front of the building, only turning when I heard Bainbridge enter. She was not alone.

"Ah, I'm sorry I kept you waiting so long Mercedes. Something has come up. Perhaps I can call you later?"

I looked at the handsome stranger with her. He looked in his mid thirties and just an inch shy of six feet. He had chestnut brown hair, a taut body and a rugged face. I hoped that this was going to be my first assignment. *Yes, thank you very much. Of course I'll fuck this guy. Hell, I'll pay him.*

He examined every inch of me with his brown eyes.

"Is this one of your escorts, "he asked Bainbridge?

"Mercedes has not started here yet. She's a new member of staff"

"Staff? Yeah, sure," he snorted as he looked at me once more, the contempt visible through his sneer. "I'm not asking for a date Ms Bainbridge. I'm not into women like that thank you. If you could please just answer my questions?"

Hey, I'm in the frigging room. Who is this arsehole anyway? I take it all back; I don't want to fuck him anymore. Give me a gun and I'll shoot the bastard in a heartbeat.

He looked at Bainbridge again. Whoever this was, he was serious. "I insist that I have the details and contacts of every member of-" he lowered his head and smiled, "who you call staff."

"That won't be a problem, Mr Sawyer. But as I have pointed out, Mercedes has arrived after the issue you refer to."

"I do not think a girl's murder is an issue Ms Bainbridge. This is a police investigation. If you do not give me the information I ask for, then I will make sure a court order is issued and we'll turn this place upside down."

Bainbridge gave a brief nod, and grimaced through her pursed lips. There were no goodbyes or thank you as he turned, leaving Bainbridge standing at her office door.

"Please Mercedes, don't take any notice," Cordelia Bainbridge said turning towards me. "There was an unfortunate incident last week. One of our staff had a drug problem. It is sad, and had we known about it, we would have helped the poor girl. As is usual with such things, it looks like it had gotten her into some trouble. But it has nothing to do with what we do here."

Yeah, right bitch. Of course not. Quarterly medicals and you failed to find any drugs in Connie's bloodstream. She was lying. She had to know Connie wasn't on drugs. Was she covering for someone I wondered? Well, at least I understood who the guy was with the charming personality. Police are easy to spot by their never-failing ability to win over the public.

Reigning in my temper that threatened to burst, I picked up my bag. "Do you get a lot of problems from the police?"

"No. We are fortunate to enjoy the protection some of our clients provide. They are high up on the food chain of bureaucracy, if you know what I mean? I'm sure they would not want their names coming to light in any investigation."

I bet they don't. It got me thinking though. *How high up the chain were her clients?*

"You have signed the confidentiality agreement now, so remember, and do not repeat what you have just heard. Anyway, I'm looking forward to seeing you on Saturday night." I could well imagine Bainbridge was. Perhaps she wanted to sample my pussy directly. The thought of Bainbridge fucking me with her tongue sent a shiver through me. It was a horny idea, but she'd be the one in for a shock. I didn't do submission that easy.

I was escorted back to my car by security. Bainbridge's guard wasn't taking any chances. He didn't want me doing any more walkabouts through the house. Leaving me at my car, I watched as he left, retreating back to the house.

"Sex pays well, I see." I looked up as I was just about to get into the Audi. No surprise to see the not so friendly detective pull up in his Volkswagen and pull down his window.

"Please spare me your outdated male perspective and policeman morality."

"There are better ways to make a living." His eyes locked on mine. This was one intense guy.

"Thanks for the advice. But I'm OK." I could buy and sell men like this ten times over. I pulled myself up short before I let loose a verbal tirade. It wouldn't be wise to attract too much attention at this stage, especially from the police.

"Look, I'm just trying to help. I've already seen one of your lot on a slab in the morgue."

One of my lot? God save me from this moron.

"She was a lot like you, except, you're breathing and she's dead."

My throat felt thick at the thought of Connie. He was right about that. She was dead.

"Yeah. Well, I'm fine," I replied, trying to keep the emotion from my voice. "I'd of thought you would be better employed trying to find her murderer than harassing and insulting escorts. Or is that what you get off on?"

With a slight smile he looked down, then right back at me. "That's the most common thing I have noticed with you high class hookers. You all seem like poor little girls who never got enough attention from Daddy, then claim prostitution is OK, but all it is, is some kind of emotional compensation."

Fuck you. But I could not help but think he was right. *Was that why Connie ended up here?*

"Take this poor girl I'm investigating now. She had no-one. Just a sister somewhere, who has just upped sticks and vanished. Didn't give a shit that her sister was murdered."

I wanted to shout that it wasn't true. That I was her sister and I did care.

"How can you know that," I asked with an even tone despite the crimson rage that was building up inside me?

"Well, where is she then if she cared so much?"

Right here you idiot. I shrugged my shoulders. There was so much I wanted to say, but without blowing my cover I had to remain tight-lipped. Nodding, I averted my eyes from him and got into my car. I didn't turn as I heard him speed away.

By the time I got back to the apartment, tears were streaming down my face. I hadn't cried since I was a child. Even when I found our mother dead in bed that morning it had not affected me. Maybe this is what you get for holding everything in. Sooner or later it has to come out.

After showering and changing. I checked my phone. Everything I needed in Connie's file was on there. I just needed to print it off. I looked out of the window again, relieved to see no black Ford Focus parked. I could not be sure who had been tailing me, if indeed anyone had, but I couldn't take any chances. Anyone could have broken in the apartment while I was out and bugged the place. I dared not ask Hugo for a sweep. That would have been asking too much and I could not be bothered checking every time I came in for bugs - it would take hours.

As I just finished zipping my coat, the Beethoven tune wailed from my phone.

Picking it up, I looked at the caller display. *Hugo.* "Oh, hello. I'm just on my way out. I'll call you in a minute."

I heard him agree then hang up.

I didn't take the car. Who knows if Bainbridge's security man had put a tracker on it while I was inside? I walked down the residential streets. The leaves had started to litter the pavements. Summer was definitely over. I pulled the phone from my jacket pocket, hitting Hugo's number. "Hi, it's me. I don't want to talk in the apartment. It may be bugged."

There was a pause on the line followed by one of Hugo's trademark sighs. It was never a good sign. "I don't know what you have got yourself into Chas, but I have just had an interesting conversation."

"Who with," I asked?

"A detective inspector Nick Sawyer from Thames Valley. He put a trace on the number of your car. I got a call from '5', telling me one of our cars had flagged up in a search. Lucky for both of us, your cover still stands."

"What happened?" I was curious. The detective knew I'd only just started. So why target me?

"I have just got off the phone from him. He tracked me from your file."

Bainbridge must have given him my details.

"He thinks I'm your old boss at the computer company," continued Hugo. "I'm not happy about this Chastity."

"He's just fishing," I replied, trying to allay his concerns. "I wouldn't worry about it Hugo. You know how important this is to me?"

"Well, whatever you have said to him, Chas, he's got it in for you. Is there anyone you don't piss off?"

Chapter Six

I was not sure what kind of tail I had on me and I needed to print off Connie's file. Taking my phone to a copying shop to print it off was risky. Their printers are always state of the art and have a memory on their hard disk - they would leave a trace.

Deciding to walk to the nearest PC World, I'd buy one instead. I could not take the chance. Someone was watching me. But who? There were only three options that sprung to mind. It could have been '5', or Security at E. Of course, it could also be Connie's murderer.

Kicking my shoes off as soon as I got through my front door. I pulled the band from my hair, letting it spill over my shoulders. I opened the carrier bag from the computer shop, pulling an extension lead from its wrapping. Plugging it in I dragged the cord to the bathroom.

Taking my other two plastic shopping bags with me, I pulled the door as close to shut as the power cord would allow me. Inside the spacious bathroom, I took another package, ripping open the plastic and cardboard. I took the screwdriver from it and taking a chair, I stood atop. It took me moments to open the light fitting. Good, no bugs. I followed the same action with the power sockets. The bathroom was clear. If I was being watched and bugged, the bathroom was safe.

I plugged the printer into the extension lead and loaded the drivers onto my phone. Loading up the printer with paper, I reeled off the documents I'd earlier scanned in Bainbridge's office. I sat on the cold marble floor with the printer next to me. When it had finished printing off Connie's file, I read each sheet thumbing through them with gusto.

She used the name 'Angel', and had worked for the agency for seven months. In the last 8 weeks before her death, she had been booked out to a client called 'Prince Fakhir' every weekend. I checked her medical details. All was in order, but no mention of her pituitary condition. She omitted to tell anyone about it. It didn't surprise me. Connie was not one to point out her flaws, regardless if they were personality or medical ones. I whistled under my breath as I saw how much she was earning. It made my salary look like pocket money compared to hers. Not that it did her much good in the end.

I took another look at the sheets, and then tossed them into the sink. Taking a lighter from my pocket, I set one sheet alight. One by one all the papers caught fire until they were reduced to nothing but ash. Scooping them to one side, I filled the sink and watched as everything turned to mush. No one would be recovering any information from that lot.

After cleaning up my mess and placing everything back in the bags, I left the bathroom. I dumped my bag of watery, charred remains into the trash. There was just one thing I wanted to check.

Outside the road was quiet. No black Ford Focus. I walked along the tree lined street, taking out my phone.

"Hey Hugo. I need you to run a check on someone."

"Don't say please. That would be hoping for too much Chastity."

"Please?"

"What is it," said Hugo?

"Can you run a background check on a Saudi Prince? His name is Fakhir? It looks like he booked Connie out on a regular basis. Every weekend in fact."

"It'll take a few hours. I have a meeting for the heads of the department to attend first, but I'll get back to you."

"Good. I have to go shopping anyway. It appears I need a dress for tomorrow night. Thanks Hugo. I owe you."

"Yes," he replied. "You certainly do Chastity Black."

I was told the Saturday evening shindig was formal wear. I was no great shopper. In fact, it bored me to death. When it came to having to stomp around stores, I knew what I wanted and treated any shopping expedition as a military operation. Get what you need, buy it and get the hell out of Dodge.

I spent the next couple of hours traipsing around Bond Street. Looking at overpriced dresses, I decided on a long red number along with shoes and handbag to compliment the colour. Before I reached my Kensington apartment, my phone beeped. It was a missed call from Hugo. Hitting the redial, Hugo picked up first ring.

"Hugo, that was fast."

"It was easier than I thought," he replied. "Your Prince flashed up immediately. Seems '6' have had an eye on him."

So MI6 were interested in him. Things were going to get trickier. As though it wasn't complicated already. I'd have to keep a low profile in case '6' recognized me. "What do they want with him," I asked?

Hugo cleared his throat. "He first came to their attention in Baghdad, less than a year ago. He was spotted with a well known Middle Eastern terrorist from one of the splinter groups over there. '6' think he's funding them or providing them a link with arms and weapons dealers."

"Do they have any evidence to support his link to the group?"

"An old IRA arms dump was found less than 12-months ago. Our guys were on their way to a military base with it when they were hijacked close to Liverpool. There was nothing cutting edge or high tech in the haul, just your average Kalashnikov and assault rifles, and the odd M5 submachine gun. But they've been recognised since and seen with this group in the Middle East. Someone here organised the hijack and sold them on. If the Prince's sympathies do lie with this group, he could easily be connecting terrorist cells with arms dealers here."

"Bloody hell. Maybe Connie saw or heard something?" It was starting to look like it.

"It makes sense. What are you going to do," Hugo asked?

I could hear the concern in his voice. "Wear my new dress and smile."

I spent the following day at the hair and beauty salon. It took less time to bug and stake out a target than it was getting dolled up for a party. From what Hugo had said, Prince Fakhir had a strong security presence who accompanied him everywhere. With any luck, he'd be there with them at the party. This was my chance to scope the other girls, the clients and the Prince and his people.

After checking myself in the mirror, I smiled. I looked good. I felt for the pins in the back of my bun. My hair was secure. 'Well Chastity Black, Carla Blake or Mercedes, or whoever you are tonight, it's time to dazzle," I told my reflection. I would be in need of therapy after all this or I'd end up forgetting who I was. Somewhere I was a psychiatrist's wet dream.

The cab pulled up outside E's gates. One of Bainbridge's' security guys looked at me then waved us through. We pulled up outside the house as a footman hurried over to open my door. Cordelia sure did like to give a good impression.

Chapter Seven

From the faint music that came from inside, it looked like the party was already underway. Bainbridge stood in the hallway. She looked amazing. Wearing a backless blue dress, her chocolate hair fell in layers. It was hard to see her as the severe taskmaster that she was.

"Good evening Mercedes. You look exquisite," she said.

I nodded and complimented her on her dress. I wasn't lying, she did look fabulous. Taking me by my arm, Bainbridge led me up the grand staircase to a function room. The room was large with soft lighting. A bar stood at one end of the room, leather sofas scattered throughout. In the other corner was another staircase leading above to another deep gallery.

As my eyes adjusted to the light, I could see there were already a number of women and quite a few men in black tie milling about talking. It looked all so dignified. It was hard to believe that these escorts were paid to have sex.

In the corner with the serving staff was Childers. She had tried to fit in. Wearing a floral ball gown, she looked more like a school mistress than someone who worked for a top-class escort agency. Along with two waiters and the bar staff, were Bainbridge's security goons. I smiled at her meaty beefcake bodyguard who had spotted me snooping. At least I still had my sense of humour.

"Here," said Cordelia as she passed me a champagne flute. You'll be introduced to everyone as the evening wears on. But for now just relax and enjoy.

I thanked her then averted my eyes to the rest of the room. There were fifteen girls in total including me. I spied the mouthy brunette from our induction. She looked beautiful, but the scowl on her face told me she felt different. In the corner at a small booth, there were a lot of men. A few were different - they were dressed in less formal attire than the other men in the room, wearing shirt and ties instead of dinner jackets. They were wearing wires. *These may well be the Prince's security,* I thought. I could not see beyond them as the three men made a formidable wall of hiding their boss.

Bainbridge roused me from my thoughts by touching me on my arm with the lightest brush of her hand. Guiding me to a middle aged gentleman, she held my wrist.

"Ah. Sir Felix. Please let me introduce you to our newest recruit," said Bainbridge. "This is Mercedes."

"Charmed," he said, taking my hand while looking into my eyes. He looked every inch the letch he was. Typical fifty year old gentrified middle aged bloke. He looked at my cleavage, making no secret at hiding his lusty gaze.

"If you could just excuse me a moment," I said. I had to get away from him. "I need to powder my nose." Well, what else could I say? Tonight I needed to find out how the agency worked, and who the clients were, specifically Prince Fakhir.

It was difficult to get close. His security team were well versed in procedures. Just when I thought Sir Felix was about to accost me again,

I managed to see the dark, swarthy man behind on the sofa. There was no mistaking it. He had to be the Prince. He donned the usual white pants, long linen shirt and a Gutra on his head. He was younger than I expected - in his early thirties and handsome.

Flanked by three girls, I could understand what they saw in him. Apart from his money, he was one hot guy.

Feeling his bodyguard's eyes on me, I turned. The rest of the room consisted of similar men to Sir Felix - too much money, repressed wives and not enough sex. I watched as the girls guided E's clients up the flight of stairs to the gallery above.

The function room was emptying fast. In the dark corners I watched a petite blond emerge with a silver haired client. His mouth pulled into a grin as he was led up the staircase by the girl, disappearing from sight as the bang of doors echoed down to me.

I was picking up the not so subtle overtures of the remaining men in the room. One good looking man with short black hair and a wolfish grin began walking towards me taking long strides. If this was in another setting, say a bar or a club, I could well have taken this guy home and fucked his brains out. There were worse men in the room I could get saddled with. But Chastity Black does not fuck on demand. Sex is always on my terms.

I was getting the drift. Tonight was not just about introductions, it was about performance. We were expected to take part in a fuckfest with these guys.

I ignored the dark haired thirty year old and walked over to Bainbridge. She was talking to Elizabeth Childers and her security guy in hushed tones.

"What's going on," I asked her? My voice sounded small. I didn't like it. I had never felt vulnerable before. Under the many eyes that rained down on me from the available men, I felt alone and naked.

"Ah, it's just a little sweetener," Bainbridge replied, giving a small wave of her hand. "Like I said, this is how we introduce you to our clients. They need to know who and how you are, if we are expected to book you out." she nodded dismissal to Childers and the minder.

Fuck. No one mentioned I'd be having sex tonight.

I was not the only one looking nervous. As my mind worked out the best option to deal with the situation, I saw the inquisitive brunette in the fake Choos'. She looked scared out of her life as she pulled away from Sir Felix.

I was good at thinking on my feet, not as good as on my back, but all the same, an idea came to me. As I looked across at the men left, I spotted one that looked the least threatening. He was only young and as I smiled over at him he blushed. I couldn't believe he had gone red. This would work well for me. Before anyone else had a chance to proposition me, I took my chance with the shy guy.

"Hi there," I said as I took him by the arm. "I'm Mercedes. You have a name?"

The poor guy looked at me as though I was about to eat him whole, bones and all.

"Charles Montpellier the Third." He took my hand and shook it. "It's a pleasure to meet you Mercedes." He had that perfect English accent that accompanied a good pedigree.

Wow. This guy was the real deal. Posh public school name and shy as a newborn kitten. Perfect. I looked at the table beside him. There were enough empty champagne flutes and whiskey tumblers to imply this guy had drank a lot already. This could just work.

"Would you like to come with me Charles? I think we are meant to go upstairs?" I took his hand and led him, swinging by the bar first, where I picked up an open bottle of Cristal and another two glasses.

Upstairs was another maze of corridors. It looked like a hotel with its doors flanking the wide landing. Some of the doors were open and I had to stop myself from laughing out loud. We passed Mr Good Looking and his wolfish grin getting sucked off by a curvy blonde with fake boobs, and a long haired redhead. Charles blushed a deep crimson as he watched. I figured there was a lot of that here. The guys like to be watched. I stood mesmerized as I watched the redhead take his full length in her mouth, while her blond partner licked at his balls.

I glanced down and saw the bulge in Charles' pants. He may blush at what he was seeing, but boy was it turning him on. I pulled him along by his hand. Near the end of the corridor stood the Prince's three security staff. Sitting at a table near the door, they looked odd as they drank tea and talked. I bet these men were used to these functions by now. One of the guards shot me a look. There was something about him that sent a cold jolt through me.

As I got closer, I noticed the Prince's door was also a little ajar. It was enough for me to get a good eyeful. Were Mr. Wolf Grin had the pleasure of just two ladies. This naughty Prince was greedy, as I eyed three of the girls with him. I didn't linger as we walked passed. I tried the door next to Fakhir's. It was empty. I closed the door behind me, taking Charles to me, kissing him on the lips, my tongue searching the depths of his mouth.

"Here, let's have some champagne." I took the bottle and poured it into the glasses. It was a good vintage. Cristal had always been my favourite.

"I don't know," he said. "I've had too much to drink already. I wouldn't want to let you down... you know." He pointed to the bed.

God, I could have laughed out loud right there and then. This guy was just too sweet. "Relax," I told him. "I know what I'm doing." That I was sure of.

While fixing our drinks I emptied a small amount of sedative into his glass. For an MI5 girl, carrying a little around in ops with men, always gave me a sense of control. It wasn't a large dose. I just wanted this guy to sleep a little. I passed him his glass.

He swigged the liquid in one gulp. *Good boy*.

"Why don't you take your clothes off," I asked him? I eased him out of his jacket, then his pants. By the time I got to his shoes he was swaying. Any time now I thought as I watched his eyes struggle to stay open. Within moments he was lying on the bed fast asleep. I pulled off his boxers. For a shy guy he had little to be bashful about. He had a sizeable dick, even when flaccid. I took a condom from my bag, ripping open the foil. Stretching the rubber I laid it next to Charles on the bed. Good if he wakes, he'll wonder what happened.

I pulled off my shoes and opened the door. Fakhir's security men were still at the table. I went back into my room and took the champagne bottle, then emptied it down the sink in the en-suite. Taking the empty bottle I left the room, making my way down the stairs. Fakhir's guys paid me no attention at all. Good. From my vantage point on the stairwell I could see right into the Prince's room.

I watched as I saw him observing two women licking at each other with eager tongues. It was two dark haired women. It was hard to see where one started and the other began. Another blond was sucking his massive dick as he watched.

"Make her cum. I want to see you make her squirm with your tongue," he demanded.

One girl got from underneath the other as she positioned herself between her partner's legs. I couldn't help but feel my own dampness as I watched the prostrate girl getting tongue fucked by the other. I carried on watching until I saw the girl lying down arch her back as she came screaming. Her fingers holding the mass of dark hair between her thighs. As her cries subsided, I saw the blond suck Fakhir with rapid swallows until he came down her throat. Pulling out he started spurting his hot cum all over her face and breasts. I watched; sweat dripping from my brow as I realized how horny it was making me. His head lifted. He looked right at me as he sprayed the blond with his jiz. He knew I was watching. How long did he know I was there?

I would need to give myself a good rub and a couple fingers when I got home. My pussy was dripping from what I had just seen. It was on fire.

I took the empty bottle to the bar, replacing it for a refill. Everything else in the gallery was quiet, apart from the occasional moans coming from behind the doors. Back inside the room, I watched Charles toss and turn. He'd be waking up soon. It was time to be done with this and get on my way. I was just about to wake him, when a loud knock on my door roused him instead. I threw a sheet over him to spare him any more blushes.

"Come in," I shouted to the door.

It was Bainbridge's pet Gorilla this time favouring a black suit rather than his brown one. He looked fierce as though he had been chewing a wasp."

"Ms Bainbridge said it's time to say Goodnight to the client. And you're wanted immediately in the boardroom."

I nodded to him and watched him close the door. Charles was looking around. He looked lost.

"Wow, you were brilliant. You are the best I've ever had," I lied.

"Really," he asked? His eyes widened and his mouth hung open.

"Don't you remember? You took me every which way. You screwed every orifice in my body. I'll be masturbating to it for ages to come when I'm alone." I picked up the condom next to him. "You better get rid of this." I handed it to him.

Charles looked at it. He could see it was empty and he was confused.

"I can't believe you forgot. God you must have been drunk. You came right down the back of my throat."

He seemed happy with the explanation. I mean, hey, who am I to rain on this guy's parade? A nice little bit of confidence would do him the world of good. "Now, I'm afraid I must ask you to leave."

I walked Charles downstairs and to the front door. Bainbridge's bodyguard was waiting for me.

"You have to come with me right away." Before I had a chance to say anything, I felt his muscular hand grasp my arm as he took me to the boardroom.

Inside the large room, all was quiet. Despite the fifteen girls from the agency crammed around one table, they were sombre. Their eyes cast downward. What the hell was going on? I didn't like it.

Moving towards the exit seemed futile. Bainbridge's charming black-suited ape barred it.

"Thank you for waiting girls," said Cordelia Bainbridge. I could not mistake the ice in her tone.

"What's this about Cordelia," one of the girls asked?

"Unfortunately, something is wrong tonight," continued Bainbridge. "It seems we have an impostor in our midst."

Chapter Eight

I held my breath. How on earth could she have found out so soon? I looked at Bainbridge waiting, but she was focused on the leggy curious brunette; the one who had a liking for designer fakes.

"In fact, you are not who you say you are, are you Ms. Bryce?" Cordelia Bainbridge's eyes burned fierce. I exhaled, relieved that Bainbridge was not addressing me, but the brunette. I was surprised she didn't turn into stone on the spot. Cordelia had one mean look.

"What do you mean," the girl replied?

"What I mean, Ms Bryce," continued Bainbridge. "Is that you are not who you say you are. You are in fact an undercover journalist for a well known tabloid, no less."

"That's ridiculous. Whoever told you that is lying."

With a steady hand Bainbridge opened a manila folder that was lying on the table in front of her. Taking the photocopies from within, she tossed them across towards the brunette. "So how do you explain that?"

I strained my eyes as I caught a quick glimpse of the papers. I was relieved that it was her that had been caught out and not me. There was a photograph of Dana Bryce next to an article she had written that had been published a year ago.

"Like I said, Ms. Bryce at your interview, we are careful with the background checks." Nodding to her head of security, Bainbridge sighed. "Carl, could you please escort Ms Bryce from the premises? And before she leaves please retain any mobile phone. She may have a recording device."

"You can't do that." Dana Bryce stood, her knuckles resting on the table. "That's stealing. You are not allowed to take any of my personal things, nor give me any kind of body check. I'll have you done for assault and theft." She straightened up folding her arms across her chest thrusting her chin out.

Bainbridge sighed. "You signed a confidentiality contract at your interview. You have no rights on this subject. It was in clear terms that all employees, regardless of what name they use are tied to all confidentiality and contract clauses. This is none negotiable and without any exception."

"I don't care. I'm going to blow this whole prostitution ring wide open." Dana Bryce spat the words at Cordelia. "The public have a right to know what goes on here. There are too many high profile clients they should be told about."

Brushing aside an imaginary loose hair, Bainbridge snorted. "You would be mistaken if you think your editor would be able to run with this particular story."

"It's not just this one angle though, is it," continued Dana? "What about all the other underground dealings that have gone on through E. Escorts. I'm sure even Special Branch would be interested in some of your transactions."

I couldn't help but stare at the journalist. What information did Dana Bryce have on E?

There was something else she knew. If Special Branch had a stake in what was going on at E, it could lead me to Connie's killer. I looked at Dana. I would have to speak to her as soon as it was safe.

"I think that's enough. Carl take her to my office and carry out the necessary checks. I'll be along shortly when I've finished saying Goodnight to our employees."

Wearing her posh dress, Dana pulled away from Carl. At least now I had a name for Cordelia's bodyguard. Stomping from the room with Carl in tow behind her, Dana complained at maximum volume. They were not pleasant names she was calling him. I understood how she felt. He had all the charm and grace of a trained Rottweiler on a chain. It was only when I heard Bainbridge's office door slam that silence ensued.

"I'm sorry you had to be party to that Ladies." Cordelia turned to us, her eyes passing our faces. "But I thought it would serve some purpose if you could see for yourselves how thorough we are here." She looked at me, a smile forming at the corners of her mouth. *Did she have her suspicions about me?*

"Now I'll bid you all a good night," said Bainbridge as she turned to the door, holding it open. "I'll be in touch soon to arrange your client appointments. Despite Ms. Bryce's efforts, it has been a successful evening and I hope you enjoyed it. Thank you."

We all filed out of the boardroom. Whispers followed each of the girls as they discussed the events they had just seen. They seemed as surprised as I was. As we made our way to the main reception area Childers looked nervous as she rang the cabs from her desk. It was obvious they wanted us out as fast as possible.

Dana had not come out of Bainbridge's office and I was loathe to leave before I had a chance to speak to her. I hung onto the last, watching each of the girls leave when their taxis' arrived. Trying to attract as little attention as possible, I tiptoed towards Cordelia's office. Loud shouts came from within and I could hear both Bainbridge and Dana, but I could not make out what they were saying.

I stood outside for five minutes waiting for Dana to emerge. When it looked like that was not going to happen, I knocked on the door. It swung open.

"Ah, Mercedes, you're still here," said Cordelia surprised to see me standing there. "I thought you'd be long gone by now."

Yeah, I'm sure you did. "I just wondered if I could have a quiet word about tonight?"

Bainbridge was giving nothing away with her face. She stood upright, pulling her shoulders back "How can I help you?"

"I just wondered if tonight is typical of what to expect? I know you are busy, but it wasn't what I had thought." *That's it Chas, play little girl lost.*

"No, it was just a taster evening, pardon the pun. Your dates with our clients are a lot less informal and much more relaxed. You have nothing to worry about Mercedes. You behaved beautifully tonight. Now ask Miss Childers to call you a cab, and I'll phone you tomorrow."

Bainbridge returned to her office. The door closed too fast for me to get a view of what was happening inside.

At her desk, Childers hung up the phone. "Your cab will be here in five minutes."

The jungle drums were fast in this place. Bainbridge must have called her on the intercom the moment she shut her door.

I wasn't ready to leave, though. I needed to speak to Dana Bryce. It might take too long to set up a meeting, and besides, I didn't want to divulge my true identity to her. As a reporter she would find a new angle to run with the story through me. No, I needed to speak to her under my alias.

There was still no movement from Cordelia's office when my cab turned up. I got into it relieved it wasn't attached to E's private hire account.

"Where to Miss," the driver asked as he swung around the central driveway?

"Could you just wait outside for a while on the road. I want to make sure my friend gets into her cab safely?"

We pulled up on the street. I'd gotten the driver to sit off a little way down, out of view from E's security cameras. It didn't bother him; the metre was running so he'd get extra. Besides, I offered him an extra tip for being so agreeable.

From my vantage point, I could see Nick Sawyer's Polo parked up. He had to be watching the place. What else would he be there for? If he saw me in the cab, he wasn't making any move towards me.

We were parked up ten minutes when a black BMW emerged from the gates. Pulling up, Carl got out of the passenger side, his heavy head bobbing on his muscular neck. Opening the door to the back seat, I watched as he pulled Dana Bryce out. She was struggling with him, and I laughed out loud as I watched her slap him across his face. She was not happy with these new turn of events. She snarled at him as she pulled away from his grasp. I felt my heart thumping in my ears as she ran from him, darting across the road. In an instant she was in the path of an oncoming car. It took me an instant to recognize the vehicle - a black Ford Focus. The poor girl didn't see it and before she had a chance to react, she was thrown onto the bonnet and flung into the road. Before anyone had a chance to do anything, the Focus sped off, not even pausing as it rounded the street corner.

Chapter Nine

I didn't waste a second and ran to the scene. Dana Bryce's body lay twisted and broken on the cold tarmac. I was not alone. Carl sat on his haunches beside her, feeling the pulse in her wrist and then her neck. Nick Sawyer was kneeling beside him, his mobile phone out.

"Ambulance on corner of Cedar Oaks- Road traffic accident. One person in immediate need of medical assistance."

He raised his head, acknowledging my presence.

"Is she alive," I asked?

"Barely," said Nick. "It doesn't look good." He flashed me a look.

Carl stood; he held his head in his shaking hands. "You saw what happened? She just ran out."

Nick and I passed a look between us. We'd seen it all. Carl was right about that. Dana did indeed run out in the road. But it was clear the girl was under considerable stress at the time. If Carl had not tried to restrain her, she would not have run away from him.

I knew the protocol. The police would want a statement from all witnesses present. Carl would be fortunate. There was no disputing she ran into the road, and anyway, he had DCI Nick Sawyer as a witness.

"Why were you restraining her?" Nick looked at Carl. His eyes gave nothing away and it was hard to read what he was thinking.

Carl looked at me for the briefest of moments. *Yeah, bet you wish you were nicer to me now, don't you asshole?* Realizing I was also a witness and my statement would get him off the hook, I was pleased to see him squirm.

"I was escorting her to her taxi. She was an impostor, an undercover journalist."

Nick looked at me for confirmation. I raised my eyebrow, shrugged, then nodded.

"You saw what happened," argued Carl. "I didn't do anything. I was just escorting her off the premises."

I couldn't argue with that. But what about the Ford Focus? I'd gotten the number plate. Observation was second nature to me. I took in information without even knowing I was most of the time. Well done MI5 for your excellent training program. It was the same car that had been sitting outside my apartment. There was more going on here than just a hit-and-run.

I looked at Carl with a new suspicion. Was he part of it all? One thing I'd learned in the field was to trust no-one and suspect everyone. I could only rely on what was in front of me and the facts. It didn't look too good from where I was standing.

Dana Bryce knew something and whatever she knew had gotten her killed. Somebody wanted her silenced. If she did pull through, I wouldn't be talking to her any time soon that was for sure. I picked up her bag. It had been flung nearby during the hit. Tucking it under my arm I waited, feeling the cold night breeze whip around my bare shoulders.

Nick looked at me. He gave the bag a fast glance. This guy didn't miss a trick. He was going up in my estimation. Maybe he wasn't as dumb as I had first thought?

I was glad that my statement was taken by a pimple faced officer. The only questions he asked were about the incident. I'd neglected to inform them on the number plate of the car that hit Dana. I'd be investigating that avenue myself.

Within thirty minutes the real circus began. Ambulances, paramedics and police cars suffocated the small tree lined street. I didn't see Bainbridge or Childers appear for a ringside seat. I was about to hop into the back of a police car for a ride home when Nick Sawyer sauntered up to me. He was a big guy, but if this was his attempt of intimidating me, he would be sorely disappointed. I'd tackled and brought down bigger than him.

"The bag if you please?" He held his hand out.

With much reluctance, I gave it to him. I watched from the back of the car as we drove off. He dug around inside Dana's purse. He was going to be further disappointed as I held her keys firm in my hand.

At the apartment I changed into jeans and a

sweater. Pulling down my hair, I scraped it back into a pony tail then wiped the bright red lipstick from my face with a moist wipe. The last thing I wanted was to look conspicuous.

Outside, the night air had grown colder. I pulled my zipped hoody closer to me. Taking out my phone I hit Hugo's number.

"Jesus Chas, do you know what time it is?"

I heard Hugo clear his throat.

"Did I disturb a night of passion?"

"Unfortunately, there are no nice men on the scene at the moment. All the good ones are already taken. I doubt this is a social call Chas, so what is it you want?"

"Are you near your laptop?"

"Why?"

"I need the address of a journalist - Dana Bryce."

"Could it not wait until the morning Chas?"

"No, I need it now," I said cutting in. "It's important."

"Usually you go for the direct approach. Why not ask the journalist yourself and make an appointment?"

"I would do Hugo, but I doubt she may be alive in the morning. She's just been hit by the same car that has been sitting outside my flat."

There was a pause as the line went silent for a moment.

"OK, give me a minute," replied Hugo. I could hear the concern in his voice. "I'll phone you back in five."

I took my own keys and with a quick look around the deserted street, got into my Audi and waited. It was only a couple of minutes before Hugo rang back.

"It's flat 2, 5 Hetherington Avenue, Camden."

"Thanks Hugo. Sorry to have woken you up. I just need one more thing. I need you to run a PNC on the car." I reeled off the number to him.

"I'm not going to be able to get it to you until tomorrow. Just be careful Chas. You've got yourself into something. Keep safe my dear."

I turned the phone down to silent and put it back in my pocket. It didn't take me as long as I thought as I entered the centre of Camden. Parking in the next street, I walked along the pavement, keeping close to the houses to avoid detection. There were a couple of drunken students and the odd car, but nothing that gave any alarm. Dana's road was quiet as I entered her building.

It was a converted town house, sprawling over four stories. I could well imagine Dana entering through the same door each day. I let out a sigh. I doubted she'd ever return to her home again. She had multiple injuries and internal bleeding. There wasn't much hope she would last until morning.

The house was deadly silent. I winced as the stairs leading to her first floor apartment creaked. Dana's flat was off the main landing. Taking her door keys from my pocket, I slipped the key into the lock. I was relieved to find no alarm. Shutting her door behind me, I took my phone switching on the torch app. The hall lit up in shadow, casting a ghost like glow. I moved with well-trained eyes around Dana's apartment. It was smaller than I expected, but neat and decorated with taste. I looked at the photographs on the wall of Dana at her graduation with an older man and woman. They must have been her mum and dad. They would be getting a phone call shortly and the world would collapse around them. My stomach flipped as I understood how they would feel. But the best thing I could do for them was to get answers.

The living room was furnished with simple pieces and looked tidy. It didn't take me long to find her laptop. As I picked it up unplugging it, I saw a buff folder beneath it. Opening it, I had seen what Dana had been up to. Inside were photographs of Prince Fakhir, his security personnel along with reports of times and places. Flight details and a picture of his yacht nestled within. As I stuck them inside my jacket, zipping myself up, I felt something fall to the floor beneath me. Picking it up, I was looking at a DVD in a plastic wallet. Keeping it with the laptop and folder inside my jacket, I took one last look around Dana's apartment before walking to the door. As I was about to open it, I heard the faint creak of the stairs. Someone was on their way up. I retreated into the kitchen and sidled up close besides the large fridge.

From where I hid, I could just hear the pins in the lock before the door opened. Whoever it was, was a professional, they had picked the lock in only a minute. I watched as two hooded men passed the kitchen door.

It was too dark to see any features, but one was a big guy and his partner was smaller with a much slighter build. One pointed to the bedroom while he entered the living room. I heard the furniture scrape on the wooden floors as they ransacked Dana's flat.

Biding my time and only when I felt it was safe; I slipped out from my hiding place and slid through the open door. Remembering to skip the creaky stair as I took two steps at a time, I left the front of the house, but not through the gate. Instead, I hopped over the neighbouring bush. I landed in the next property's garden, then around the side and back out onto the street. If anyone was looking out of Dana's flat, they would not have seen me. Inside the Audi I took the laptop, folder and DVD from my jacket, placing them on the passenger seat next to me.

I was still cautious when I arrived back at my apartment. I took my phone out again shining the light at my door. Good. The inch of fishing wire I'd placed across the door and between the frame had not been disturbed. It wasn't an MI5 trick, but something I'd seen in a movie. It worked for the character so I adopted the method for myself. It had never let me down.

I took the folder into the bathroom while kicking off my trainers. Inside I found a number of sheets on Prince Fakhir. They appeared to be a report on his movements and times. There was a dossier on his flight times in and out of the UK dating back a year and a picture of his luxury yacht. It wasn't telling me anything other than something was going down with the Prince. It was what I'd already suspected. There were no typed or written notes in the folder. I could only hope that whatever Dana Bryce was onto was on her laptop. I needed more to go on.

Taking the DVD from its case, I pushed it into the machine and hit play. It was a filmed recording of the Prince on his yacht. From the angle of the camera, it looked like he was being filmed in secret. Lying on a large round bed, the Prince was fucking a girl from behind while kissing another. His mocha body glistened with perspiration as he plunged into the pussy of the girl in front of him kneeling on all fours. He had a beautiful cock, long as well as thick. There was no sound to the recording, but you didn't need to lip read to know what the Prince was saying. If he knew he was being filmed, he didn't show it and he was not camera shy.

I recognized the two girls with him. They were two of E's escorts who had attended the party that evening. I watched as I saw Fakhir fuck the blond with furious thrusts before pulling out and coming into the other girl's mouth. The two women were not putting on a show. I could tell from their expressions, that they were getting as much out of the experience as the Prince was. I watched as their mouths contorted and their eyes begged for sexual release. Wow, this man knew how to make the most of things. I could imagine what his cum would taste like. I watched his hot fluid hit the back of the girl's throat. It dribbled down her chin, while the blond he had just fucked kissed it off her dark-haired partner.

The camera moved as I saw the Prince beckon to someone. It had to be the secret photographer. If I could only see who was doing the filming, it might give me something more to go on. I gasped as I watched the tall leggy blonde in black stockings and underwear walk in front of the camera.

She leaned over pouring the Prince Champaign in a cut glass flute. I would have recognised that heart shaped birthmark on the thigh anywhere. It was Connie. I moved forward towards the TV as I watched her sip from a glass, a bittersweet smile on her face. This was the same smile I saw on her at our mother's funeral.

I reached my hand out to touch the LCD screen. She looked into the camera, as though she was looking straight at me. It was Connie filming the Prince, but why? Was she planning to blackmail the Prince, and how did Dana get hold of it? *What did you get yourself into Connie,* I thought as I sat watching the screen? I paused the DVD and looked at the beautiful face of my kid sister. I wiped the bitter tears from my eyes. *I'm sorry Connie, I let you down.*

Taking a minute to catch my emotions I unpaused the DVD. Both Connie and Dana had been targeted by the same people for what they knew.

I took the stolen items of Dana's and hid them in the wall safe. I'd move them in the morning to a secure location. I was in a safe house, but who knew how safe it was?

I got into Dana's laptop easy enough, but there was no reference to Fakhir, E Escorts or Connie. The folder had bits and pieces. Most of the emails and documents referred to the Prince's movements while in the UK and the people he met. Whatever else Dana Bryce had come across that involved Fakhir she had not written it down anywhere. I didn't think it was because of the sex tape. The Prince was not what you would call discreet and as a man in his position, that sort of thing was expected. No, there had to be something more to it.

It was getting light outside before I made it to my bed. In normal circumstances, I fell asleep with little trouble. You learned to rest when you could in the field yet light enough to wake at the least noise. But Connie's face haunted me before sleep finally claimed me. And then there was DCI Nick Sawyer involved in the loop. Could he have had anything to do with it? Could he be involved somehow? After all, he'd been parked outside E's headquarters all night watching. Perhaps he was watching to make sure Dana Bryce was hit and to provide a cast iron witness statement for Carl? I had more questions that needed answering. I wanted to trust Nick Sawyer and I had no idea why.

Chapter Ten

I'd finally dropped off just as it was getting light outside. I've learned to get by on little sleep, but I felt the soft cotton beneath my bare skin and clung to it. It was just typical that as I drifted off, my door buzzer shrieked, bringing me back to the land of the living.

More annoyed than wary, I threw on some jogging pants and a vest and padded my way to the door in bare feet, wincing at the feel of the cold laminate floor. I would have thought an upmarket gaff like this would be kitted out with underfloor heating.

I looked at the visual display unit connected to the camera on the doorstep. DCI Nick Sawyer was looking right into it. It was like he knew I was there and was conveying his annoyance via the screen. He did not look happy.

I hit the intercom. "You have got to be kidding me. I've only just closed my eyes," I said.

"I still need some questions answered about last night."

You and me both pal. I buzzed him in. Looking at him through the lens for a moment, he looked like he was another one who hadn't slept at all.

Deciding to get it over with I let him in, pressing the entry access to my unit. I left my door open as I went into the kitchen. I needed coffee. I wasn't surprised he didn't knock. He walked right into my apartment. I flicked my head at him and nodded to the kitchen diner. "Coffee?"

"Yeah. Thanks. Black no sugar."

I carried our mugs over to the table. He was watching me. He was wearing the same jeans and navy blue polo shirt he was wearing the night before. His brown eyes dug into mine for a brief instant as they flickered over my body. I wasn't wearing anything under my vest. It was a chilly morning and my erect nipples were visible under the sheer cotton of my top.

His eyes told me nothing. Cold and relentless, he opened a folder.

"I gave my statement to your officer last night. I don't know what I can add to it," I said.

"Want to tell me what last night was all about?" Running a hand through his thick chestnut hair, he took my statement from the folder and a pen from his pocket.

"What do you mean?"

"Stop playing with me. I spoke to the driver of the taxi you were waiting in. I watched you myself. Do you want to tell me who you were waiting for?"

Thank God, this man didn't decide to go into medicine instead of the police. He had one hell of a bedside manner. "I was curious about Dana. I wanted to see what was happening. I was just being nosy."

"So take me to the beginning. What happened last night that resulted in Dana Bryce being escorted off E's premises."

I sipped at my coffee. Its bitter taste felt acidic, and my mouth dry. "Why don't you ask Cordelia Bainbridge and the other staff present? They know more than I do."

"I already have-last night, Miss Blake. You are not the only one who hasn't had any sleep.

I'm tired and want to get this over with, so if you don't mind." He rested his elbows on the wooden surface and opened a notebook, pen poised.

If I wasn't annoyed before, I felt the rage bristle somewhere inside me. Who did he think he was barging in here treating me like a suspect?

"Have you found the car and the driver that hit Dana," I asked?

Of course he hadn't. It was a professional job. Whoever hit her was too good to be discovered.

"We're still on it."

Not wanting to reveal how annoyed I was, I sat back and relaxed in the kitchen chair. "It was an introduction party with some clients. Bainbridge called us into the boardroom and exposed Dana Bryce. As it turned out, she is an undercover journalist."

"Was. Ms Bryce died two hours ago."

I cast my eyes down-wards in case I gave away my feelings. Another young woman dead, no doubt because of what she knew.

"Like I said DCI Sawyer," I continued, "I was curious. I asked the cab driver to wait. I wanted to see what happened to Dana Bryce."

"So you were worried about her?" He looked up at me, his eyes searching.

For the briefest of instants, I could see hidden warmth in his gaze.

"And it's Nick."

Wow. A little informality from the man himself. I was surprised. "No. I just told you. I was curious."

"What else was said at this meeting? Did Dana Bryce disclose any other information?"

"No. She was indignant, sure. But nothing surprising."

Nick looked through my statement. He drank the coffee, taking long and slow sips, letting the silence hang between us. I knew what he was doing. I'd been trained the same. If you allow an uncomfortable silence to spike it makes the interviewee need to fill the void. *Sorry pal. It's not going to work on me.* I sat back and smiled.

"Is there anything else you might have forgotten to tell the officer last night?"

"You were there yourself. You saw it with your own eyes," I replied. "Dana Bryce ran out in the road. She was not pushed. Shouldn't you be looking for the hit and run driver instead of questioning me?"

"I think you know more than you're letting on Ms Blake."

Of course I am. But he doesn't know that for sure. Besides, I could not trust him. If I told him about the Ford Focus, he'd go after it like a hammer on eggshells and drive the culprits into hiding.

"So what are you saying," I asked him?

"Two women are dead. Both suspicious circumstances. Both connected to E Escorts and I don't think it's a coincidence."

"So what do you think is going on?"

"I think it is deliberate, premeditated murder. And you Ms Blake can help me find out why."

I stood up scooping both our mugs taking them to the sink. My fingers brushed his hand by accident. It was the smallest and briefest moment, but it sent a jolt of electric pleasure through me. It was momentary, but I could tell by his eyes, he had experienced the same chemistry from the brief touch. I could not jeopardize my cover by revealing everything to him. He eyed me, penetrating my depths with his glare. He was different to the normal plod I'd dealt with. Sure, he was hot. I could see the strain of his muscles under the fabric of his brown leather jacket. He was intense with a darkness about him that sent a shiver through me.

He did not take his eyes from me as I turned and thought his offer over. He licked his full lips as he waited for my response.

"What makes you think I can help you?"

Nick looked around the apartment. "You're already in the viper's den. Think of it as not just sex for money, but for a good cause. Who knows, it might even make you feel better about what you do for a living."

"When you put it in such charming turns, it makes it difficult for a girl to say no." This guy knew how to talk himself up.

"If that was you lying in the morgue, wouldn't you want someone to care?"

I did care, more than he would ever know. My heart was breaking and I dared not show it. My sister was dead and I had let her down.

"Do you have family Chief Inspector Sawyer?" I had gone back to his formal name. First names were addressed to friends. Nick Sawyer had made it crystal clear he was no-one's friend. Especially not mine.

"No."

"Must get lonely," I replied. I'd hoped I'd hit a nerve, but with someone like DCI Sawyer you could never tell.

"In a job like mine, it's a bonus. I don't need anyone."

His face was like stone. Cold and hard. I did not believe him. Everyone had something that weakened them at least on an emotional level. In my experience in the field and undercover it was usually the coldest ones who hurt the most.

I folded my arms and with designed defiance lifted my chin up and looked down my nose at him. I was not going to be a pushover, but I could not afford to have Nick Sawyer on my case either.

"I'm not taking any unnecessary risks, though," I answered. "If I do find something out, I'll call you. But it's not like I'm trusted at E. I've only started. Me and Bainbridge are not on close terms. It's not likely she's going to divulge girly confidences to me."

"Just do what you can. Someone like you must be good at screwing over people to get what you want - one way or another."

His cruel words did not sting as he had hoped they would.

"If you don't mind me asking, there is something I wanted to ask you?" Nick said. He stood up. He bent his head to look at my face.

I was only a few inches smaller than him, but standing there in front of him, I felt tiny. "Why is it that when someone asks, 'if you don't mind me asking,' they ask anyway, even though they know they are going to offend someone?"

He didn't blink and remained silent for a moment longer than was necessary. "It's just that you don't seem the type of girl to fuck men for money. I suppose I wondered how you got into prostitution."

He was not pulling any punches, but it was a stark reminder of what Connie had gotten herself into. "Tell me, Nick, how many men sleep with women because they just want to fuck them? Do you think men care about the feelings of women when they are shagging them? So why not get paid for it? At least it's honest. Women lie back all the time and spread their legs and get fuck-all in return."

"You're wrong. Not all men are like that." His eyes bore into me.

"I'm just telling you that's the way things are."

"No," he replied. "That's the way you are. You have a distorted view of men. Someone must have hurt you in a bad way to feel like that."

I could have slapped him there and then. Not because of what he had said, but because I knew he was right. I did not respect men. I had felt nothing for them. I had never had a serious relationship and I had never loved a man."

I went to the door and opened it to him. "Is any of this relevant to your investigation," I asked?

"No."

"Then please mind your own business."

Turning to me before he walked out he passed me his card. "I'll look forward to getting word from you soon."

I let the door slam behind him. Half of me wanted to punch him, the other half, to kiss him. Why was I letting a man get to me like this?

Chapter Eleven

It must have been late afternoon. I was asleep when the pay-as-you-go mobile bleeped me awake. The sun was fading as I sat up groggy, my hair falling across my face.

'Missing you and wanted to say hello. Call me.' It was a text from Hugo.

I showered quickly, throwing on a pair of jeans and a clean blue Kronk T-shirt, before I grabbed my leather jacket and headed out onto the street.

Leaves covered the tree lined road, and the autumn chill promised winter was not far away.

"Hey Hugo," I said when he answered on the first ring."

"The PNC on the ford focus drew a blank Chastity." Hugo coughed, clearing his throat.

"According to the database the plate belongs to a Vauxhall Corsa and is owned by a Mrs Jane Ellis, who died this year age ninety-eight. So unless she's a mastermind criminal who's faked her own death before switching plates, we have nothing to go on."

I gave a little chuckle. I had missed Hugo's dry sense of humour. "I hear you get senile as you get older, perhaps she just forgot."

So someone had exchanged the plates with the Ford Focus. I was not surprised. It would be gross negligence for these guys to make it so easy for them to be traced.

"I have no idea," continued Hugo, "but someone is covering their tracks well. And they must have access to the PNC database to switch this kind of info. At first it didn't come up. It was only when I noticed the dates didn't tally that I dug deeper. So I'd add computer hacker genius to the list of criminal activities."

I was not getting any breaks. I ran a hand through my hair. It was still damp from the shower. "I'll just have to do it the old fashioned way. Legwork and savvy."

"Any more news about your journalist mole."

"She's dead Hugo. Someone went to great pains to silence her. DCI Sawyer was around my place this morning sniffing."

"Anything I should know about?"

"Well, he is suspicious and he's determined to get answers. He thinks Connie's and Dana's deaths were deliberate murder. I can't argue with him there."

"Do you trust him?"

"I don't know. I'm not sure if he's for real or if he's part of it all and just trying to find out who I am and find out what I know. He's fishing without any bait all the same. He did ask me to help him dig a little for him." I pictured the haunted look on Nick's face that morning. Trying to figure out Nick Sawyer would be like cracking open a golf ball. Impenetrable exterior with layers upon layers underneath. Even the lines around his eyes looked dark and foreboding. But I didn't underestimate him. Friend or foe, he was intelligent and relentless with it.

"Tread with care on this Chas. You have stumbled into a rats nest and it's protected by some top level people."

"I had already gathered that some of E's clients are distinguished in our chain of command. Has '6' come up with anything?" I had not seen anyone that looked like secret service at the previous evening's party.

"They're still onto the trail of your Prince. But there's a large business deal happening with our Government and the Saudis. They need to be delicate. It's worth billions to our Country's economy. Orders are not to upset the apple-cart under any circumstances. So what are your feelings about this detective? Do you think he's part of it all?"

I hoped not. Out of all the men I'd come across and after all the disappointments, I wanted Nick to be the real deal.

"I don't know," I replied. "You'll just have to watch this space."

I had just hung up on Hugo, when the phone rang again. It was Cordelia Bainbridge.

"Good afternoon Mercedes. I trust you are well today? I heard you witnessed that unfortunate incident last night."

Unfortunate? What drugs was this woman on? It was more than unfortunate. Witnessing someone being driven into was just about as bad as it got. "Yes, it was pretty grim."

"Of course, despite our feelings about Ms Bryce, we are devastated at what happened.

Carl Standish was distraught. The poor man feels guilty." Bainbridge paused, her voice faltering. "Of course, as someone who witnessed it yourself, you know it was not his fault."

More like Cordelia's security man is afraid of being implicated in murder. "No, you're right. She ran out into the road under her own volition. I gave a statement saying as much to the police."

I could almost feel the relief in her voice through the mobile connection. "Thank you. However, I'm calling you on more positive grounds. Do you remember the Saudi gentleman from last night?"

"Yes?"

"His name is Prince Fakhir. He is a prominent member of the Saudi Royal family and also a particular well-thought of client of ours. Anyway, to cut to the chase, he's having a party on his boat tomorrow evening and has requested that you join him."

"Wow. That's great." *No shit it was great.* But why had he asked for me? Was he aware of whom I was?

"It seems he was taken with you last night, but was unable to enjoy the presence of your company. But he specifically asked for you by description. You must have made a powerful impression on him."

"I think I remember him. Where and when is this party happening?" I pursed my lips together. I needed to get as much information on him as possible.

"His yacht is moored on the Thames by Oxford. You're expected at 8pm. I'll send all the details to your phone. If you keep the Prince happy, you will enjoy repeat custom and he's known for his generosity to his girlfriends.

"I'm looking forward to it. Is there anything else I should know about the Prince?" *Like is he a terrorist or a murderer?*

"He likes his women to do what they are told. But that won't be a problem for you."

Me? Submissive? I almost laughed into the phone. I doubt there was a submissive bone in my body, but if it meant finding out who killed Connie and why, roll me over and take me, I won't complain. I would take on any role if it meant meting out justice to the son-of-a-bitch who killed my sister.

Chapter Twelve

I threw a final glance at my reflection in the full length mirror in my bedroom. I looked good. I knew it. I felt a little more relaxed. I had a few hours shuteye and been able to stash Dana's laptop, DVD and paperwork in a Paddington Station locker. It was sometimes used by '5' for dead-drops. It would be safe there until I needed to return for them.

Checking the clock on the dresser, I reminded myself to get my arse into gear. I would have to get a move on or I would be late. The instructions were that I arrive at the dockside at 7.30 pm sharp.

Checking my lipstick was fixed, I picked up my purse. I was wearing an elegant silk Japanese dress. When it came to men, they didn't have a clue what they liked. Most women think to look sexy they need to reveal as much of their body as possible. Put it all on show. I knew when it came to seduction and power in the bedroom, it was about teasing. Show them something, but not a lot and they would salivate to see what the rest of you looked like. It was all in the anticipation.

It was almost dark when my cab pulled up at the quay. Fakhir's boat was moored at the end. After paying the cab driver, I walked along the side. I couldn't have mistaken the Prince's yacht. It was by far the biggest and most expensive boat there. The gang plank was down when I arrived adorned with a plush red carpet that ran all the way up to the entrance. I was met by a black suited security guy. He was wearing an ear piece. Of course Fakhir was royalty, security would be strong. I only hoped they dropped their guard when women were around.

"I'm expected." I stood upright and stared at the bodyguard in front of me. He wasn't the biggest I'd seen, but he had a wiry ferrety look about him. I didn't like him.

"Name?"

"Mercedes."

He looked through me then brought his hand to his ear. It was blustery on the Quayside, the wind was whipping up. Whoever he was communicating through his comms must have had trouble hearing him. He turned his back on me before I heard him say my name. Turning back around, he nodded to me.

"Please come with me. Prince Fakhir is awaiting your arrival."

He escorted me onto the boat. I knew it was massive, but I had no idea how big it was. It was decorated in regal hues. Not tacky as I thought it would be. I always thought that Saudis had a gaudy taste when it came to decoration. Gold taps, and all that, but this was beautiful. Fakhir's security man escorted me below, where I was met by a corridor. Paintings adorned the walls and I felt my heels sink into the sumptuous red carpet beneath my feet. Towards the end, Fakhir was waiting. He smiled as I approached then waved his security guy away.

The Prince looked as handsome as I remembered. His long silk shirt emphasised his sleek but muscular body well. He was not wearing his headgear, and his face seemed somewhat more chiselled than before.

"Good evening Mercedes. I was so pleased when Ms Bainbridge confirmed your attendance."

I smiled as he held his arm out and ushered me into the room.

"Thank you," I replied. "It was good of you to invite me."

"May I say how beautiful you look. Since the other night, I have not been able to get you out of my head."

Same here, I thought, but not for the same reasons I bet.

"It was such a pity that I did not get to meet you then. I would have loved to have gotten to know you better. But at least now we can get to know each other."

I felt a little uneasy as we entered his private suite. I recognised it as the same room in Connie's film. There were sofas and a lounge, but the Prince took me straight to the bed. It had to have been custom made. It was gigantic and could have held up to five people in comfort. It probably did, knowing this guy's sexual appetite. After all, I had seen him in action.

"Will it just be the two of us this evening," I asked?

"Unfortunately not. I have some business contacts that will be joining us later. I've also asked for a few other girls from your agency to join us. They will be received by my guests. But I wanted to spend a little time alone with you first." This was going to get tricky. Even though this was one hot guy, with one of the nicest cocks I'd seen in some time, I wasn't sure I wanted to let him fuck me. "I am honoured Prince Fakhir," I lied.

"No, it is me who is honoured. You have me intrigued. Please tell me a little about yourself. You were born in Britain - is that correct?"

Was he just fishing, trying to pretend to be interested, or did he have any suspicions about me? It was hard to tell.

"Yes."

"And family?"

"Yes." I didn't feel like elaborating.

I took the offered champagne from the Prince pretending not to notice as his eyes ran up and down my body. I looked about his suite only turning my attention back to him, when I had collected my thoughts. "And you Prince Fakhir. Do you like Britain?"

"Very much," he smiled. "So many pleasures here."

I tried not to flinch as Fakhir touched my shoulder, his fingers running down my sleeveless arm.

"You are here a lot I think?"

"As much as I can. But I do have to attend business at home at times. I wish it was not so, but I do have to travel. Matters do not attend to themselves."

"Being a Prince, you must be busy and in constant demand." Yes I was making small talk. Anything to put off the inevitable.

"Yes. But what would life be if you could not enjoy the pleasures it has to offer from time to time."

He moved closer, taking the glass from my hand and placing it on a marble table.

"Enough talk for now. Take your clothes off Mercedes. I wish to look at you."

The warmth and feigned interest in his eyes were replaced with fire and lust. This was a man who was more than used to getting what he wanted. I pulled the zip down at the side of the black silk dress, ensuring care was taken. Other than wanting to draw things out, I wanted him at my mercy and drunk on lust. His eyes took in every action. I pulled the dress over my head and let it land beside me. I was standing in just my underwear.

"Beautiful. Now your underwear, leave only your stockings on."

I licked my lips as I continued with the eye contact. Unfastening my bra, I pulled it away from me allowing the Prince a view of my breasts. On some level I must have been horny, my nipples stood erect surrounded by their large brown areolas. I touched them with long slow strokes, making the Prince gasp.

"Your panties Mercedes. I wish to see it all." His exotic accent was hypnotic.

I hitched my fingers into the black silk sliding them down my stocking clad legs. My hairless pussy completely revealed. I saw the Prince bite his lip as he began towards me, his fingers outstretched as one hand reached for my pussy, the other my breasts. He was just about to kiss me when the ringing phone behind him interrupted him. He paused as the ringing trailed off and stopped. His fingers probed my inner lips finding my clit. I could feel myself getting wet. Whatever was happening to me, his hands were driving me wild. They sought deeper into my folds before a finger, then two inserted into me, this time making me gasp.

As I felt myself give into the wave of pleasure, the phone sprung back to life. This time the shrill tone caused the Prince to sigh and pull away.

"A moment please," he said before putting his finger into his mouth and licking my juices off. He smiled before he picked up the phone.

I stood regaining my composure. He had only just touched me and I could feel myself about to orgasm, with just his finger. I listened as the Prince spoke into the mouthpiece.

"I told you I did not want to be disturbed." The Prince turned around walking out into the bathroom. I could just about hear him. His annoyance obvious in the manner he spoke to his caller.

"Is it not something you can handle yourself?"

I was picking up just one side of a conversation. But perhaps it was important.

Little else was said before Fakhir returned to the room.

"Excuse me. Wait for me here. I will be back as soon as I have dealt with a problem. Pour yourself some more champagne. I know how you ladies like it so."

Before I could nod, he was gone. The door shutting within seconds. He looked like one frustrated Prince as he stalked from the room.

I put my dress back on taking a long towelling robe from the Prince's bathroom and wrapped it around me fastening the belt. I crept from the room ever watchful. I had no idea how long I had to scout the boat, but I knew I had to take any opportunity offered to me. From the deck I could hear music and voices filter down to me. I looked up and down the corridor deciding which way to go when I heard footsteps. Sprinting back to the Prince's room, I sat down on the bed, grabbing the champagne flute just as the door opened.

Standing in the doorway was a security guard - 6 feet tall and just as wide. He pursed his lips before he spoke. "Prince Fakhir sends his apologies. He has requested you stay in his quarters. He will return later."

I nodded, showing little interest. But I was busy taking in every characteristic about this man. I had seen him before at the introductory bash at E with the Prince.

He was British and had that military thing about him. I'd seen MI5 officers recruited from the armed forces conduct their manner the same way. There was something about this guard though. His black hair looked velcroed on, his suit without a single crease and he seemed devoid of any human emotion. I took a distinct dislike to him immediately. There was something cold and deadly about him. And I'd seen my fair share of killers and madmen in my time.

I'd have to be careful and give it a little time before I went walkabout again. The Prince's guard did not look like the forgiving type.

I began searching the Prince's quarters. Drawers, cupboards and anything I thought might be of interest. Apart from the wow factor at the pure magnificence of Fakhir's quarters, there was nothing. His business and other paperwork had to be held elsewhere. It did not surprise me. No doubt the Prince's bedroom saw a lot of action and he would never leave personal papers on view for the hired sex to ogle.

Opening the door to the corridor was risky, but the silence was both reassuring and frightening. Taking slow steps I edged my way along, looking into the rooms I passed.

When I ended up at the foot of the stairs, I climbed up the steps. The music was louder from here and the sound of laughter and voices drifted along to me.

Once on deck I tiptoed along, keeping out of sight. As I came to the lounge, the music was playing at full volume. I took a chance and looked through the window. The curtains had not been closed. I recognised a couple of the girls from E's introduction night, except not in the positions they were in now. Four men were taking one brown-haired girl. Her hands held two cocks. She was sucking one as she lay spread eagled on the floor, a half dressed man in just a shirt was fucking her pussy. The Prince wasn't joking when he said he was entertaining guests. The men did not even look up from their prize as their faces contorted in what looked like either agony or pleasure. It has always been difficult for me to tell those two emotions apart during sex.

On a sofa another girl was being spit-roasted by another two men. She was screaming, asking for more. When they pulled out of her pussy and mouth, I gasped at the size of their cocks. If they had come near me with those two huge things I'd have slapped them away.

I was a little discouraged that the Prince was not there, which meant he was somewhere else. I'd have to be careful as I searched the boat. The last thing I needed was to run into either him or his beefy scowling bodyguard, who made Carl from E look like a pussy cat.

As I edged away from the fuckfest, I made my way towards some other rooms. One looked like a security hub. There were a couple of flat screen monitors. In the corner on a phone sat the Prince's security guard. I could not hear what he was saying, but he was shouting. I could just make out his raised voice above the wind that was picking up and distorting their words.

There was something about this guy that worried me. Taking my phone from the robe's pocket, I held it up by the window and waited. As the guard turned I hit the button taking a picture of him on the phone's camera. I slid behind a post, sending it to Hugo. I wanted to know more about this guy. If MI6 were monitoring the Prince, then they must have a file on his guard.

After making sure the Prince's guard hadn't made me, I began snaking my way past the glass doors of his office. The next room was what I had been looking for. I was rewarded. A huge teak and gold desk took up most of the space. It dwarfed the laptop sitting on it. Making the most of the opportunity, I closed the door behind me. Within a minute I had gotten into the Prince's laptop. I looked through his drawer. I found a flash drive and plugged it into the USB port. It took me no time to get passed the encryption code and start downloading the Prince's files. While it was downloading I carried on rifling through his papers and drawers. There was nothing of interest in his paperwork, but as I came to the last drawer of his desk, my eyes settled on something I recognised.

It was a gold necklace with the letter C pendant hanging from it. I would have known it anywhere. Connie had taken it from me when we were teenagers. I had bought it, but she would take it whenever she had the chance. It caused huge arguments when we were kids. In the end I relented and let her have it. I held it up between my thumb and forefinger. It was broken - snapped through its gold links, as though it had been ripped off. It was the proof I had been looking for. Connie had been on this boat. She would never have left her necklace behind - that much I knew. But was Connie on this boat the night she was killed? Pulling the Prince's diary from his top drawer, I flicked through the pages. There were two entries for that date; one for an Embassy bash in Chelsea, the entry below had been scribbled out with black ink. I knew what it meant. Connie was on the boat the night she was murdered. In the same fashion they had dealt with my sister, they had erased any evidence.

E had denied she was booked out that night. They lied and someone had deleted the appointment. I checked the laptop, the Prince's files were almost seventy percent downloaded. It was going too slow, if I got caught like this, I'd follow the same fate as my sister. The final files were downloading and the progress bar was at ninety nine percent. There was not enough time, though. I heard the footsteps and recoiled in horror as the door began to open.

Chapter Thirteen

I whipped the flash drive from the USB point, ducking immediately behind the polished desk. The door opened. I would be found any minute and had no excuse for being there.

What could I say? I'm doing a bit of role play with the Prince? A kinky variation of hide and seek. Nope, I didn't think it would wash.

I began running scenarios for an exit strategy through my mind when I heard a phone ringing. At first I thought it was mine. Holding my breath, I felt in the robe pocket. I'd put my phone on silent. The ringtone wasn't coming from my handset. I have only been that stupid once before on an op and it almost got me killed. I would never make that mistake again.

It was Fakhir's scowling guard from below. I recognized his deep voice immediately as he answered his phone.

"Yes, everything can go as planned. How can anything go amiss now? All the problems have been eliminated."

I wondered who he was talking to. Whoever it was, had given me a slight reprieve through their perfect timing. I listened as the guard paused presumably while he listened to his caller.

"No, I have no reason to think she is snooping. She's down below in Fakhir's suite."

It took me a moment to realize he was talking about me. But who the bloody hell was he talking to? And who knew I was there? It had to be someone from E, but who? Carl? Bainbridge?

The call was pulled up as a voice from outside shouted. I heard the Prince's guard tell their caller they would be in touch. I was breathing with relief, and slumped back against the cold wood of the desk as I heard him turn around and leave. So far so good. I was safe for the time being. At least I had one piece of information - Fakhir's guard was in on something.

I edged around the desk and was relieved to see the office door closed and the room empty. It had been a close call. With the flash drive wedged between my cleavage, I kept low and made my way to the window. The deck was clear. Being careful not to be seen I opened the door ajar first and checked, then made a quick exit, finding my way back to the steps that led below.

As I got near the Prince's room, I was pulled up short.

"You, what are you doing?"

I knew the voice. After all, I had only just heard it on the phone in the Prince's study. "I was getting lonely down here all by myself." I tried to sound tipsy and stupid like a drunken teenager on a prom date.

The oversized man studied me. His eyes drilled into me. I knew that look. It was the look of doubt. He was musing over the fact that perhaps I was snooping.

"You were told to wait in the Prince's room."

"I've been waiting on my own for ages," I whined like a brat. "I thought I'd been forgotten."

"Go back and wait. The Prince is greeting an important guest."

Wasting no time I made my way straight back to Fakhir's room. Taking the flash drive I dropped it into the lining of my purse. It was all getting a bit too close for comfort. That exit strategy would come in handy just about now, I thought. When I was working in the field, I had a team I could rely on. Here on my own I had no one. There was no risk assessment undertaken and I had no idea what to do should things turn bad.

I took my phone and texted Hugo. I keyed in the yacht's location, asking him to cause a diversion so I could get away without arousing suspicion. I had just deleted the text I had sent and placed the phone back in my bag when Fakhir breezed into the room smiling.

"Now my sweet girl. I am sorry to leave you for so long, but now we can resume where we left off."

At the sound of his exotic voice, my skin tingled. In any other circumstance, I would have relished fucking this guy. The thought that he may have been involved with Connie's murder, turned me cold.

He hadn't noticed I had dressed. Instead he came over to me putting his hand across my back while he began kissing the side of my neck with gentle lips. I felt a shudder as his tongue caressed my skin. I turned looking into his mocha eyes alive with lust and mischief. My body was saying yes, my integrity and reason screaming no. Before I could yield, I was aware of a commotion coming from somewhere close. The immediate rapping on the door shook me from my sexual torment. The Prince sighed, upset at the interruption.

"What is it," he demanded as he called back to the door?

"Your Majesty, we believe your safety to be compromised."

I recognized that deep voice. Had Fakhir's guard made me? At first, I thought I had been found out, but came to my senses as I heard sirens in the distance.

Fakhir looked at me. It was bittersweet and a part of me was disappointed, the other relieved.

Opening the door, I saw his guard at the threshold.

"The police have had a report of a man climbing aboard this vessel dressed in black, masked and carrying a duffel bag. We need to remove you to another location your Majesty."

I watched the exchange between the Prince and his head of security. No doubt the tip off to the police was via Hugo. I was indebted to that man, he seemed to know me better than I knew myself.

I gathered my coat and bag. I didn't need to be told that this was my exit. Fakhir turned to me.

"It seems, my dear Mercedes that fate conspires to keep us apart. I vow I will see you again soon." The Prince bowed his head to me, and I realized that despite all his bluster, this man was respectful of women. His security man on the other hand, snorted as he stood aside to let me pass. Now this was a man of little respect for anyone, perhaps even to the person who pays his wage. Of course, I had already decided I did not like him and was almost certain he had some hand in Connie's death.

"Callaghan, show the lady out and make sure she arrives home safely." Fakhir threw me one last sad smile. I could not imagine this man being a killer, but I had been wrong before.

I walked along the corridor to the steps leading up on deck. I could hear voices above. Hushed whispers along with a few uniformed officers talking to Fakhir's staff. I was conscious of the Prince's man behind me. His Majesty had called him Callaghan, but again I doubted it was his real name. I hoped that once Hugo had put his face through the mix, I'd know more about the guy.

"You know, you don't need to see me home, I can call a cab." I did not want to spend any more time in this thug's company. I rounded the steps before I felt the night breeze smack my skin. In a way it felt a relief. At one point earlier, I doubted that I would be feeling anything again if I had been found in the Prince's study.

Callaghan looked at me tight lipped. He showed no emotion, his face impassive. "There's no need. Someone is already here to take you home." He nodded his head in the direction of the Quayside.

My eyes followed his nod. It was Carl. He was standing on the dock, his suit immaculate, his face like flint.

I turned to Callaghan unsure. *Were they in it together? Did they know who I was?* It was impossible to be sure. How could they know? Still, feigning a thin smile, I walked along the dockside.

"Bainbridge thought I should wait for you and pick you up." Carl didn't smile, but nor did he scowl. "The car's just a little further."

"How did you know the police were here, at the boat I mean?"

Shrugging his shoulders, Carl narrowed his eyes. "I didn't. Bainbridge just told me that it might be a good idea to wait for you. You were only booked out till midnight anyway."

"You make it sound as though I'm like Cinderella. I already have a Prince. What are you? The doormouse with a pumpkin ready to take me back to my life of drudgery?"

I knew my words had smarted him, but it felt good.

"I would not call the way you live your life a fairy tale, would you?"

Touché. I remained silent as we headed back to the car. I sat in the back while Carl drove me back to my apartment. Aware that this could be a set-up between Callaghan and Carl, I was ready to fight if need be.

When he pulled up outside my apartment building, he did not speak, he just waited until I got out. No sooner had I shut the car door behind me, I heard the screech of tyres and watched him speed off down the street. I was relieved all the same to see him leave.

I still had my doubts about Carl, but I had bigger fish to net. I needed to see what was on the flash drive and get an update on Callaghan. I was thinking of possible links between the Prince and Bainbridge when I heard hollow footsteps creep up behind me.

Chapter Fourteen

I listened. The footsteps were walking toward me. Waiting until I could hear the assailant's breath, I turned to see the figure loom towards me in the darkness.

Instinct kicked in. I hit out hard and fast punching the intruder on the jaw. I took a step back and saw him stagger backwards before hitting the ground.

"What the...?" The voice sounded stunned.

I sighed. "Oh, it's you." There was just enough moonlight to make out the features of the man I had just knocked down. "What are you doing sneaking about at this hour detective Sawyer?"

Nick rose from the floor holding his jaw with one hand. "Bloody hell that was one hard punch. Remind me not to cross you any time soon." He sounded shaken. Raising both his hands, he approached me in supplication. "I was just checking you were OK. I saw there was a problem at the Quayside. That was some boat you were on."

I wasn't going to apologise to this guy. After all it was his own fault for stalking me. I took a step forward while Nick took one back. Did he think I was going to hit him again? I had to stifle a laugh, although I was annoyed.

"It's not a boat. It's a yacht," I said not flinching. "You were following me?"

"It's my job. There are two women lying in a morgue. Both are connected to E Escorts, so forgive me for doing what I get paid for. Besides, I don't want to see you occupying a slab next to them. But don't thank me."

Did he care what would happen to me? For a moment I felt my breath catch in my throat. Was there more happening between me and Nick? I was feeling affection towards him. His admission that he cared had brought me up short.

"Where did you learn to fight like that anyway?"

I smiled, keeping the air of mystery and the good hearted flirting going. "Hey in London, a girl needs to know how to defend herself."

"Especially one in your line of work I expect." There was no camaraderie now. He had become cool and distant again.

The words stung me like a dying hornet. I looked down towards the floor, my keys hanging in my fingers. "Let me get some ice for your jaw." I was not going to let his words get to me. I wished I had knocked the bastard out.

He followed me up the stairs, where I let him into my flat. I had left a light on when I went out earlier, it threw a warm glow around the living room. "Sit while I get something for your face." I went to the kitchen and shook the kettle flipping the switch before making my way to the freezer.

As though it had reminded him of what had happened, his hand rose to his jaw. "So what happened tonight? Police got a tip off from a member of the public about an intruder seen accessing the boat."

I was about to correct him, but he beat me to it.

"Sorry, I mean 'yacht'. After all, high class escorts like yourself would not be seen on a mere boat now, would they?"

I ignored the sly dig he was taking at me. "An intruder, is that what it was," I shouted through to him? "I wasn't told." I was not great at grocery shopping and the best I could come up with from the drawer was a bag of frozen peas left by the last occupant.

I came back with the peas and a tray with two cups of tea and sugar. I wasn't sure how much Nick knew about Fakhir. I put the tray on the coffee table, then sat next to Nick on the sofa.

"Funny though all the same. While I was watching the yacht, I noticed you creeping about. Was that part of the deal or something? Does the Prince like you to creep about his boat —I mean yacht?"

The jibe had no effect on me. Lifting the bag to Nick's chin, he drew back from me wincing. I regretted hitting him so hard as I saw the bruise emerge on his face. "Don't know what you mean," I lied applying a little more pressure to his jaw. He yelped.

"What are you not telling me, Miss Blake?"

I wanted to tell him. For a moment I thought I would, but I drew back. I still didn't know of his involvement. Was he following me, or was he there anyway for some other reason? Someone was involved with Callaghan after all.

Nick looked into my eyes hard. I could feel his breath on my cheek. He was too close for my own comfort, but I couldn't drag myself away. As I went to remove the frozen bag, his hand came up touching mine. I felt the energy surge through me, tingling from every pore, every limb. I started to shake as his hand found his way to my face, his fingers brushing my skin and finding the nape of my neck. As his mouth found my lips, my body buckled. His tongue found the inside of my mouth as I kissed him back just as hard. I felt his hands around my waist, pulling me closer to him. He began stroking me outside my clothes and looking for entry into the soft skin underneath. I wanted him. Everything was on fire. I had started to pant.

Then it was over. His mouth and his hands gone.

I opened my eyes to find him sitting there, his eyes cast down-wards. He looked desolate.

"I'm sorry. That should not of happened." He looked up at me under his long brown lashes.

"But it did." I was starting to feel the tingling subside. No man had made me feel like that. What was wrong with me? Nick Sawyer was a misogynist with a black and white morality. I didn't even think I liked him.

He stood looking at the bag of frozen peas on the table. "I'd rather we forget what just happened." He looked at me with cold scrutiny, as though I was something he just trod in and was trying to wipe off his shoe. "I would not want you to think I came around here for a freebie."

"What? I wasn't thinking that." *Who the hell did this man think he was?*

"Well, whatever you were thinking, I'd be mad to get involved with a girl like you."

"Really? I think you had better leave Detective Sawyer." I wasn't going to have this man thinking he was on the high moral ground to me. I was no Escort, but even if I was he had no right to treat me with such disregard.

Nick touched his jaw, then nodded toward the window. "Sorry for creeping up on you earlier," his voice was flat. I could have been a stranger on the street. "Thank you for the tea and the ice." He spoke with the charm of a well rehearsed robotic answering machine. All warmth had deserted him, leaving behind just a chill.

I had no idea what the hell was happening. The acerbic tone had gone from him, replaced with cold courtesy.

"I'll see myself out. Thank you Ms Blake for your time."

I stood there reeling. How dare he treat me with such diffidence? I heard the door shut. Part of me wanted to run after him and explain everything, the other part wanted to hit him again.

I sat down on the sofa and picked up my mug of tea. *How the hell did that happen? Why did I let myself fall for that man? No, Nick Sawyer wasn't the mad one - I was, for allowing him to get under my skin.*

I could not let myself dwell on Nick, it would serve no purpose to let the man get to me. Taking the flash drive from my bag, I powered up my laptop and inserted it into the USB drive.

I was hoping to find something, even an odd email, a bank transfer, something. But all that was on the Prince's hard drive, were schedules for diplomatic visits, a bit of porn and some invoices from E escorts. I couldn't believe how much they charged Fakhir for our services. Bainbridge must have been making a fortune.

I checked the date of Connie's death. According to his schedule, the Prince was attending a charity bash in Chelsea. It was just I had discovered through his diary. I was finding too many questions in my investigation of the Prince, and not enough answers. Something was not adding up about this guy. Why would my sister be on his yacht if he was not there? It made no sense.

Sleeping was not easy that night. If I got two hours, I would have been happy. Instead, I spent the night running things through in my mind. I'm pretty good about work. I can switch off and let my subconscious put the dots together. But not this night.

Maybe because it wasn't work. I replayed mine and Connie's childhood over and over. I remembered pushing her on the back garden swing when we were still in Primary school. Then there were the late night chats about boys. We were close in those days. We only had each other, especially when Mother was on one of her drinking binges. I still could not believe Connie was gone. I would never be able to tell her how I felt - that I loved her.

Every now and then, Nick would figure somehow in my mind. I couldn't fathom how the man had gotten me so hot only to turn so cold. What confused me more, was that I let it affect me. My sanity was hanging in the balance - I needed to toughen up.

The light started breaking through the gap at the bottom of the bedroom blind. It was morning. I'd only had a fitful burst of sleep. In the end, I gave up trying to get any more, what was the point? It was not going to happen.

I swung my legs out of bed, yawning before I hit the bathroom. After a shower and getting dressed, I looked at the bedside clock -

8.30am. Not wanting to waste any more time. I picked up my phone, threw on a leather jacket and ran down to my car.

On the second ring, Hugo picked up.

"Yes Chastity," said Hugo. He did not sound pleased to hear from me. "I suppose you want something. Why else would you be calling me so early?"

"I was on my way round to yours. I couldn't sleep."

"I'm just waiting for confirmation about your man from the picture you sent me last night. By the way - I'm assuming you got out OK. I'll admit my diversion was a little clumsy, but I did not have a lot of time."

"Yes, it worked a treat. Thank you I owe you one."

"You owe me more than one Chastity."

I smiled and put the phone back in its cradle on the dashboard. I did owe Hugo, I owed him big time.

Hugo opened the door for me as soon as he heard me knock.

"I have two pieces of interesting information for you my girl."

I cocked my head to one side feeling my pony tail brush past my neck. It was the same spot the Nick had kissed and caressed me the previous night. At the thought of him once again, I felt a tremor run through my body.

"You OK Chastity? You look flushed."

I wasn't about to confide in Hugo about Nick, so I just nodded. "What's this information then?"

I followed Hugo into his study at the back of his house.

"Seems Fakhir's man is wanted by '6' and many other Agencies, including our American cousins."

"What does the CIA want with him?"

"He's a mercenary dear girl. He's responsible for brokering and supplying arms and weapons to a number of terrorist and splinter groups. Started out in Ireland and now has affiliations around the globe. He's a busy little bee."

"So what's he doing with the Prince?"

"That's a good question Chastity, and I have no answer for you. The Prince's sympathies do run to one known group, but I doubt he'd be involved with arms trafficking."

Hugo passed me a dossier. Inside was all the information on Callaghan. Hugo was right. He was a nasty piece of work and driven by money and greed. He had a past working with the Russian Mafia, as a mercenary in Serbia, Iraq and even in the Sudan. Wherever there was conflict and suffering this man was there creating more, all in the name of greed. "He's working with someone," I said.

"Who?"

"I think it might be someone at E. Perhaps Carl or Bainbridge. Although I'm not ruling anyone out. I heard him on the phone last night. That's why I'm here."

Hugo bowed for dramatic effect . "I'm in awe of you Chastity. That could have been no mean feat to pull off."

"What was the second?"

"What," asked Hugo?

"The second piece of interesting information. You said you had two."

Hugo rested his rump on the side of his desk." Ah, yes. I almost forgot. It also appears that your admirer Carl at E Escorts does not come up to our scrutiny. In other words, his backstory is a lie. He is not who he says he is. I had verification come through one of my sources just this morning."

It was starting to make sense. Callaghan was in cahoots with someone at E. It was beginning to fit.

I went back to the apartment. I had a lot to think over, I was getting into dangerous territory. Had Connie been killed because of what she knew? I was pretty sure the journalist was killed because of it.

I didn't take the dossier that Hugo had on Callaghan. I had a good memory and from what I had read, he had been in Fakhir's employ only nine months. He'd targeted the Prince for some reason. The more I understood of Fakhir, I saw him as nothing more than a playboy with money, a high sex drive and time on his hands. I did not have him down as an international arms dealer or terrorist - he was just too shallow for that kind of faith and commitment. So what was the Prince's involvement? I wouldn't get any answers sitting on my backside with a cup of tea. Determined to do something I got changed.

Wearing jeans, trainers and my favourite hoody, I pulled my hair back. I twisted the lengths, piling it on top and securing it with a black scrunchy, pulling the hood from my sweater over, shading my face.

I drove as far as I could to the quay, parking my car a few roads down. It was early evening and the subtle cold breeze that had built up throughout the day started to go through me. I pulled my jacket closer to me shivering on the Quayside. I climbed aboard the yacht moored next to Fakhir's, some couple of hundred meters away. It was deserted. I imagined it was a part time plaything for someone rich and bored. I watched as the daylight faded, turning grey as evening beckoned.

I settled in the lookout. From here with my binoculars I had a clear view of everywhere visible on the top deck of the Prince's yacht. It was Callaghan I was looking for. I needed more on him. If he knew he was under suspicion, he would be careful. I found some cushions and propped them up against my back on the seating in the glass cabin - it looked like I could be in for a long wait.

Fakhir's boat was quiet. I could see no one and I started to wonder if instead the Prince was not there. Wherever Fakhir went,

Callaghan was in attendance. He was the head of security after all.

After another forty minutes, I had decided that perhaps I was wasting my time. As I was deliberating about leaving my post, I noticed movement in my eyeline on Fakhir's boat. It was Callaghan. He was with two other guys - the same ones I had seen the previous evening.

Picking up my binoculars, I watched. Callaghan was on his mobile. There was only one way to find who Callaghan's consort was, and that was from lifting the phone from him and taking the data from it.

I left my hiding place and stole from the boat. The Quayside was dark by now with only minimum lighting. It was a quiet area. It had to be the desolation of the place that made the spot attractive to both Fakhir and Callaghan. Fakhir for his sex orgies and Callaghan for his arms deals.

I stayed low, snaking my way along the dock lest I be seen. There was enough coverage to keep me hidden. Thank god for small mercies. It looked like the Prince's boat was quiet. There was no entertaining and sex crazed parties tonight. I stayed out of view behind a pallet close to the yacht.

From where I was I could see Callaghan in the security room, the light from the bank of monitors glowing. I was pretty certain where I was that there was no CCTV or security equipment. Fakhir's men would be more focused on the boat itself, than the dockside and neighbouring yachts.

After what seemed like an age, I waited for the security room to empty. There was only Callaghan and another man inside. I was shivering from the cold night air when I was rewarded with my moment. I could see his phone on the console board, all I had to do was wait for them to leave. I crept along the side of the boat, picking up some large pieces of gravel that lay underfoot. With fluid movements I began hurling them at the deck on the opposite side. As soon as I heard someone shout, I ran back to my hiding place. Callaghan and his man ran from the room.

"What's with the shouting," he called?

"Someone's throwing stones boss." The voice sounded foreign and I heard Callaghan sigh, as he and the other security guard in the cabin went around to check it out. I didn't waste a second. As soon as they were out of sight, I made a run for it. I was on the deck and in the security cabin in moments. I kept my face low and well shaded, thankful I had on a sizeable hooded jacket. If they checked on the CCTV, they would think I was a man.

I saw the phone and pocketed it immediately, making a run for the dockside. I took off like a rat in a burning building, not stopping until I reached the roadside. The area was deserted, not a sound or soul to be seen. I had just caught my breath, when I heard the engine. Before I had time to react I saw it tear around the corner. It was a black Ford Focus. Shit, I was in big trouble now. I started running in the direction of a brick and metal warehouse that ran parallel to the dockside. It looked like an industrial area. The car sped up, it was right behind me. I did not think I could outrun it. *Was this it, was it over for me?* In a minute the car would be upon me and I knew it would not stop until I was dead on the cold hard floor.

Chapter Fifteen

I ran straight for the buildings. It was late, and I doubted if anyone would be there at that time of night. My breathing was heavy and I could feel my leg muscles complain and tighten as I tried to sprint faster. I rounded a corner. My heart leapt as I saw an enclosed area, fenced off from vehicles. I jumped the barrier and headed off behind a warehouse. I could still hear the Focus somewhere behind me.

As I headed around the side of the warehouse, my heart thundered, then sunk to the pit of my stomach - it was a dead end. I could hear the engine close by. As I ran around the corner, I pulled up short at the sight of the car. It was not the Focus or Callaghan but a black BMW. The passenger door swung open, revealing the driver.

"Get in," shouted Carl. He looked flushed. "I'll explain later. Just move it before they find us and we both end up dead."

I did not trust him, but neither did I have a choice. I got in slamming the door. Looking at me with a solemn glance, Carl nodded, then sped off through the warehouses and onto the road. We were clear.

"How stupid can one person be?" Carl looked at me in disgust. His hands held the steering wheel tight.

"I beg your pardon?" What was this guy's game?

Pulling down a side road and then sidling the BMW into an alley, Carl parked the car out of view from the main road.

"Don't play stupid with me. I know who you are Chastity Black. What I want to know is what MI5's involvement is with Fakhir?"

I was stunned. How the hell did he know? I was good at thinking on my feet, but I wasn't prepared for this. "I don't know what you're on about."

I flinched as Carl dipped his hand into his inside pocket of his jacket. It wasn't a gun he fished out, but his wallet. He handed it to me. I opened it while eying him with suspicion. As I flipped it open I saw it. It was an identity card. *Michael Tomes - Security Services*. It made sense.

"You're '6'," I asked?

Nodding Carl took his wallet back. "I've been working E for the last nine months and you have almost wrecked my cover, not to mention all the ground I've made up. Because of you, it could all have been for nothing." His eyes locked onto mine relentless and angry.

"OK," I said not sure how I was going to explain myself. If he had already reported me to his superiors, I would have heard by now. "How did you find out who I was?"

"Well, for a start, you don't come across as the typical escort. Something about you worried me, so I ran your face through some facial recognition software. You came up under a fair few number of aliases, and then bingo. You were associated with a cover '6' ran in Morocco. Everything after that was easy."

I shifted under his stare.

"So?"

I coughed. He would know immediately if I lied, so I decided on the truth. I told him everything. Connie, Fakhir and Callaghan. The only name I kept out of the conversation was

Hugo's. He didn't need to know. Besides, the last thing I wanted was to get him into trouble. As I told him everything, he sat there silent. I didn't want to tell him about the phone, but I had little choice. He knew I was on the boat for a reason. I took it from my jacket pocket.

"Say I believe you," he began raising his eyebrows, "why shouldn't I blow your rogue operation up to my superiors? You know what you are doing isn't sanctioned? You'd lose your job - even do a stint in prison."

I did not think it a good time to use my killer wit. Instead, I decided to be honest with him. "Because I have a sister who has been killed, and if anything, as a human being you must understand why I am doing it. Besides, won't it be better if I work alongside you. '6' would never know and I could help you. You get Callaghan and I get Connie's murderer. I could be of use to you Michael."

"It's Carl, remember. Can't afford to blow cover now."

I looked at him, cocking my head to one side. I'd had this man figured out all wrong.

"If you are going to help me then you are best using my alias don't you think? But be warned, you don't do anything before running it by me first. This is my operation, don't forget it. I'll come around to your place about 1am. I need to get back and show an appearance at E, before whoever is working with Callaghan puts two and two together. It'll give you a chance to go through Callaghan's phone and we can go through the findings together. I mean it Chastity - don't try and cut me out of it."

I let out a huge breath and smiled.

We remained in silence on the drive back to my place. Carl pulled up outside my apartment. As I was about to open the door, he laid his hand on my arm. "Now remember. Any information you pass it onto me." He passed me his card. "My number," he said.

"Thank you." I reached over and put my arms around him in a friendly hug. When I leaned back I noticed a ghost of a smile on his face.

As soon as I shut the car door behind me, he sped off. Damn, I thought. I still had to pick up my own car near the quay. But for now, I was relieved I had someone on my side.

"What is it with you?"

I turned and saw Nick Sawyer standing at the end of the path.

"You're shagging the hired help now?"

I didn't respond. There was no time to get into it with him. "What do you want Nick?"

"Well, I had come to apologise about what happened, but I needn't of bothered." He looked towards the direction Carl's BMW had gone. "Seems you are doing OK without me. To think I felt bad."

I stood defiant. I was not going to get into an argument with him on my doorstep. Neither was I going to defend myself and come across as a whining woman. For a moment I felt a pang of remorse, but Connie's murder and the case were too important to allow myself to drop my guard with this man.

Taking the keys from my pocket, I gave him a sideways glance. "I don't care and I'm not bothered what you think Detective Sawyer."

I turned to watch him walk away. The problem was, I did care and I was bothered.

Inside the apartment, I showered and changed donning sweat pants and a vest. I took Callaghan's phone and was immediately locked out. I would be naive to assume he had not put a PIN lock on it.

I didn't have the necessary equipment to break the lock. It was too late to bother Hugo, besides, I did not want to admit I'd been found out by a '6' agent. I took Carl's card, or was it Michael? Keying in the number he gave me, I shot him a quick text, *'need laptop for the phone. Locked out. C'*

I didn't have a lot of time before he would arrive, so I threw a pizza in the oven. Fieldwork always made me hungry and I realised my stomach was complaining. Just as the oven pinged, my door buzzer alerted me. As I expected looking at the monitor, it was Carl.

He walked into the apartment to be greeted by the smell of pepperoni pizza.

"I wasn't sure if you had eaten." I put the food on the table.

Raising his forehead, he smiled. It was a rare occurrence I gathered from this man. "Thanks," he replied. "Yeah, I am peckish."

I made myself comfortable on the rug while I picked up a slice of pizza. Carl sat on the sofa, taking a laptop from the rucksack he had with him, along with some cables. He put it on the table and picked up a slice of pizza himself.

"This should do it. My boyfriend Ralph is a techie for the agency. He has every piece of kit going."

Everything fitted. Carl was gay. That was why he showed no interest in the girls at the agency and why he did not flinch from the sex fests he attended. The guys from my department would have killed for a job like his.

Licking grease from my fingers, I passed Callaghan's phone to Carl. I watched as he fired up the laptop and plugged the cables into the phone and then into one of the USB ports on the device. I got up and moved around to see what was happening.

Within minutes Carl had not only unlocked the phone's PIN, but he was retrieving the data from the phone.

We looked in silence. The only texts and emails were to do with Fakhir's schedule. There was nothing untoward. No phone logs that supported my claim of his involvement with someone from E.

"Can you retrieve the deleted data," I asked?

"Same as I was thinking," said Carl wiping his fingers on his pants. "Should be easy enough." He tapped into the keyboard on the laptop. After a couple of minutes the data was there on the screen. Callaghan had deleted all the call logs and texts.

There were quite a lot of calls to and from E, and texts from an unknown mobile number. I wrote it down. I doubted they were all escort related. Everything was there. I passed the number to Carl. "Can you call this in? We may get lucky if it is a contract number."

Carl took the number and dialled from his phone. I made a pot of coffee while he was onto someone from his office. When he hung up, he gave me a grim nod.

"It's a pay-as-you-go SIM," he said. "But the last ping it gave off was at a tower - the same one that covers E's headquarters." He sat back down and reached for the laptop. "The number's no longer active. The SIM has probably been destroyed."

"Can you check the night of Connie's and Dana Bryce's deaths," I asked Carl?

His face paled as he ran up and down the log details. "Yeah, you're right. Three calls on the night of Connie's murder to and from E's office and two more calls on the night of Dana's hit and run."

Connie had been set up by someone from E and now I had the proof.

"It's got to be Bainbridge," I said. It was the obvious answer.

"I was with Bainbridge the whole time the night of Connie's death. I had to drive her to a function in Chelsea, she was there until midnight. She couldn't have made or received those calls at E if she was somewhere else."

"It was probably the same party that the Prince attended."

"That's why he cancelled his date with your sister. I checked; she was booked out to him that night, but she couldn't have met with him Chastity. He wasn't there."

"What if she wasn't told? What if, whoever set her up, sent her there knowing they were sending her to her death?"

Carl looked at me, the lines crumpled on his forehead. "You mean Bainbridge?"

I'd have to think about it. "OK Carl. There's nothing much we can do tonight, best get some rest. Maybe with a fresh mind, we'll have a better idea tomorrow. It may just be one of E's security staff who's in on it."

"I don't think so. I'm a good judge of character, and I reckon the guys there are pretty solid."

I sighed and nodded. "You get home to Ralph. God knows this job we do puts enough strain on our relationships." My mind drifted to Nick. I still had that sinking feeling in the pit of my stomach.

Chapter Sixteen

I was dripping in sweat when I woke at 5am. It was only a dream, but it shook me. I was on Fakhir's yacht and Connie was there, broken and bleeding on the deck, crying. She was asking me to help her, but I couldn't move - I was paralysed and unable to reach her.

I pushed my hair from my face and got out of bed. In the bathroom mirror, I could see I had been crying myself. I could still taste the salty tears on my tongue.

There was no point going back to bed. I was too shaken, so I flipped the switch on the kettle, while taking a tartan throw and wrapping it around me. I had to figure it out soon. Before long 5, E Escorts and Callaghan would be onto me. It was just a matter of time.

I sipped my coffee in the warm glow of the lamplight before switching the TV on. The news was always grim. I wondered why on earth I had committed to protecting this Country. Stabbings, shootings, rape... all the awful things people do to each other. At least in this day and age forensic science enabled most of the bad guys got caught and were taken out of harm's way. OK, not all - there were always loopholes.

I watched the TV in silence. I spotted one of my old colleagues who worked in Special Branch, John. He was in the background on the news escorting a foreign ambassador at his hotel. I allowed myself a snigger. John would hate that job. He always complained that these foreign diplomats got away with all sorts of things in the UK. He hated having to accompany some of them to their sordid little sex trysts. They could never get away with such things in their own Countries. Some committed crimes, but could not be touched because of their diplomatic immunity.

As soon as the thought entered my head, everything clicked. It wasn't even 6am yet, but I reached for my phone.

"Chastity? What on earth are you doing calling me so early? Has something happened," Carl asked?

His voice sounded grainy and I could hear another male voice mumble in the background.

"It's Callaghan. He's using Fakhir's diplomatic immunity to trade the weapons. That's what he's doing with him."

"Jesus, Chastity. Couldn't it have waited until it was at least light outside instead of calling me at stupid o clock?"

"If I'm right Carl, it means the weapons must be on the boat. For the amount he's trading, he'd need something big to transport them. The boat makes sense. I need another date with Fakhir. I have to get back on that boat."

Carl remained silent. I could imagine him rubbing his hair and the sleep from his eyes. "OK, I'll call you back in a bit. I reckon it's too dangerous at this stage though. Callaghan knows someone is onto him."

"Yeah, but who would suspect an escort? It's not like he saw who I was last night." That much was true. Donned in the hoody, I could have been anyone.

I was showered and dressed by the time Carl called me back just after 9 that morning. I was eating a piece of rubbery toast when I picked up my phone.

"We have another problem," he said. "Our man in the middle east believes there's a shipment due from the UK. It's not weapons Chastity. It's far more serious." Carl's voice dropped an octave. "We've just had Intel that a substance held at Porton Down was stolen. We don't know when, but it has only been noticed after our source confirmed a buyer for it."

"What is it," I asked? I knew Porton Down was the military science park and home to the Defence Science and Technology Lab. Security there was ironclad. No one could even sneak in and steal a paper-clip, let alone a biological or technical weapon.

"They call it KD-5, but it is has been labelled as the Pandora Toxin. It was created as a deterrent five years ago, but under tests there were mutations. It looks like a pink liquid, but when heated to 300 degrees it converts into a gas. Once it becomes airborne, it is ingested and kills the white blood cells while infecting healthy cells. The lungs are first to be infected and breathing becomes painful. Death is expected within 24 hours of inhaling the gas."

I could not believe what I was hearing. "How much has been stolen?"

"One vial, the size of a small thermos flask. But it's enough to kill thousands, especially if the wind is blowing strong. It could carry the toxin miles. All the security services are on high alert."

What on earth were our Government doing creating poisons that could kill so many? There wasn't time to feel indignant about it. I would ask my superiors questions later. Until then, KD-5 had to be found. "How was it stolen for Christ-sake," I asked?

"We're just trying to figure that out. The last check was three weeks ago, someone inside has switched it since."

"So there's a mole? Do you know who the buyer is?"

"Our source has located an extremist group somewhere out there. They're gathering their forces. God knows what would happen if they got their hands on this stuff."

"Who are they planning to use it on," I asked?

"We think it's us, Britain. We have the peace conference to be hosted in London in a few days. We think that's where they are going to let it loose."

"You'll have to cancel," I replied.

"Negative," said Carl. "It could be the only chance to catch the culprit. We can't afford to see them disappear into obscurity with the poison and then to be used again at a later date. We'll never get this kind of Intel on them again Chastity."

I let the information sink in. There was more at stake than just catching my sister's killer. "Then you need to get me on that yacht."

"When?"

"Tonight Carl. We haven't got any time to play with here." I was about to ring off when I remembered Bainbridge. "Another thing Carl. I need to get into E today and go through Bainbridge's things. If she's in on it, there may be something we can glean from her. Have you got enough on her to bring her in for questioning?"

"At this point, with what's at stake, it's best to leave her out there. We have her tailed. If she is Callaghan's contact she may lead us to the buyer."

I understood the wisdom behind his plan. "I still need to find out if she's involved. What do you know about her?"

"Zilch. She's private. It's not like she tells me anything."

"What about Elizabeth Childers? She must know something about her?"

Carl paused for a moment on the other end of the line. "Maybe. If anyone was to know anything about Bainbridge, it would be her. Look Bainbridge is out all day, she's not due back till four this afternoon."

"Good, gives me time to have a chat with our Miss Childers and angle my way back onto Fakhir's yacht."

We hung up. Any amount of KD-5 was lethal, especially in the hands of terrorists. I called Hugo immediately, he had also been made aware of the threat earlier that morning.

"Chastity, I never thought I would say this, but you have to find out where Callaghan plans to make the drop. It's too late to try and get someone in at this stage. Even if we bring Callaghan in now, the poison is still out there. Someone else could make the drop."

"Does that mean I'm sanctioned?"

"Yes Chastity. You have '5's backing. I'm in Thames House now. We are on alert. Everybody has been called in. We have to find these bastards before it's too late. Don't get me wrong Chas, there will be a backlash for going rogue, but we'll deal with that later. For now, they need you."

I hung up and glanced at the clock. It was time to get moving.

***

I was let in through E's gates immediately. I knew Carl was inside. When I parked my car outside the main house, he came out to meet me. He looked dour.

"I've been through the usual in Bainbridge's office. There's nothing there to link her with Callaghan or any of the terrorist community." He stood with his back to the house, his shoulders rigid. "You may have more luck finding out about her from Childers."

I nodded and walked behind Carl as we entered the house. I followed him to Childers' desk, keeping up the pretence.

"Miss Childers, Mercede's wishes to speak to Ms Bainbridge. I've notified her that she is out most of the day. Perhaps you could help her?" He gave me the briefest glance, then stalked away in the direction of the security office.

Childers smiled at me. She was wearing one of her typical dowdy outfits. A high collared gaudy purple blouse and woollen skirt that went unfashionably mid calf. It did nothing for her when matched with her purple woollen tights and sensible black flat court shoes.

"Oh, I do hope you can help me," I knew I was being sweet and gushing, and I was bloody good at it. "I wanted to apologise for the other night on the Prince's boat. Unfortunately, it was cut short. Some sort of emergency on there. I just wanted the Prince to know that I'm still available if he would like another meeting?"

"Yes of course," she said. "I did hear something about it from Ms Bainbridge."

I sat down on the chair by her desk. I noticed she looked flustered as she leaned forward.

"Well, he has asked for you again, but I haven't received details as to when." She shuffled the papers on her desk, then opened an A4 diary. "Ah," she began. "Here it is. I have the details, but no time or date."

I needed to get on that boat and invited would be easier than uninvited. "Can you call him and ask him," I said? I looked at the diary trying to get a better look at what was written. "It's just I don't want the Prince to think I am fickle and not interested. Because, of course, I am." I sounded a little too desperate. But for once it wasn't an act, I was desperate. Thousands of lives were at stake.

Childers' smiled at me. She was far more approachable than her boss Bainbridge. "I'll call him now while you're here. I don't see why he should have a problem with that. I can well understand why you would want to keep him. I am told he is generous to our girls."

Yeah, sure, I thought. *Especially considering my sister was murdered on his boat.* "Oh would you? Thank you so much." I was making myself feel sick. How nice could I be?

I listened as she picked up the phone. I still needed to find out about Cordelia. When she replaced the handset, I smiled at Childers like an expectant child on Christmas morning.

"Yes, no harm done. I spoke to Prince Fakhir himself. He would love to meet with you tonight if that is possible. I told him you would." A doubtful look passed across her face. "Of course, I was not presuming," she said, "You can make it, can't you?"

"Oh yes." I took the piece of paper with the time on it and scanned it. It was back on the boat at 8pm. That was good. But I still didn't have a real plan. I would need one.

I placed the paper in my pocket, but didn't budge from my seat. I wanted more. "So have you worked here long Miss Childers?"

She looked at me with a curious glint. It was obvious that no one paid this woman any real attention. For all her worth she may as well be invisible.

"Just under a year I think. I was here shortly after Cordelia first established E."

"It's just that you don't seem..."

"... The type of person to work for an Escort agency? Yes, but it is interesting, well paid and I get to travel. I try not to judge people on what they do. It beats pen pushing for the civil service."

"I hope you don't mind me asking, but you seem so different from Ms Bainbridge. Is she a good boss?"

Childers looked down while her fingers twitched. "I shouldn't talk about it. Cordelia does not go in for office gossip." She looked back at me and offered a wan smile. "It can be challenging at times."

"Is Cordelia married? Does she have a family?"

"No. I don't think she has all that much faith in men."

I could well understand. Neither did I. "So where do you get to travel to? You must go to some exotic places?"

"Well," continued Childers, "we haven't long come back from Abu Dhabi. We were meeting with some diplomatic clients there who are due to come to the UK soon. It was such a beautiful place."

I wondered if this is where Bainbridge had brokered the deal with the extremist group. It would make sense. "It sounds wonderful. What kind of diplomats? Like the Prince?" Childers eyed me with suspicion but I needed more information.

"No, not royalty, but high up in some Government or other. Ms Bainbridge doesn't give me all the information you see. But I had a fabulous time while I was there. I do like the warm weather." She picked her pen up and looked at me with mild curiosity.

I wasn't going to learn anything more from Elizabeth Childers, so I smiled and bid her a good day before driving back to the apartment. It had to be Bainbridge who was Callaghan's contact at E.

I had just parked up outside my flat, when I was roused out of my thoughts by a loud rapping on the passenger seat window. Staring in at me was Nick Sawyer. I felt the familiar stirrings rise in me. Lowering the window I said nothing and waited for him to speak.

"I need to talk to you."

"I'm busy," I replied. Yes, I was abrupt, but considering how this man had treated me, he was lucky I didn't punch him again. Also I didn't want him to know how he affected me on such a deep level.

"Now." He was insistent and didn't look in the mood for an argument.

I sighed. I was tired and had a lot of thinking and planning to do before my date with Fakhir. "So talk," I said.

"Not here. Inside." He stood back from the car and walked up the path to the front door.

Resigned at the fact I would just have to deal with my feelings for him and the insults he hurled at me. I locked the car and followed him, letting him into my apartment.

"So what do you want," I asked, taking my leather coat off and hanging it on the rack in the hallway?"

He walked straight into the living room and sat down on the sofa. "Answers. Something is going on, and I think you can tell me what."

"You'll have to tell me more if you expect me to give you answers. What the hell do you mean?"

Nick slipped his coat off and placed it on the arm of the sofa. "Well for starters, I tried to get a warrant for your boss. Seeing as you haven't got me any information, I put in for one so I could access E's client record."

It was true, I hadn't helped him. But in my defence I did have other things on my mind. I did have to catch a murderer and stop what could be the worst terror attack this Country had seen. "And?" With a shrug of the shoulders I hoped I'd got the message across to Detective Inspector Nick Sawyer, that I couldn't care less about him.

"Nothing. I got called into the Super's office and told to leave it. I've been pulled from the case."

A part of me was relieved. "And you think your Superintendent is a client of E's?"

Wiping his mouth with his hand, Nick paused. I could see he was giving the matter some thought. "No, not the Super, but someone higher than him, whatever is going on is way past the Super's pay grade."

I knew what had happened. It was always the same when some police officer stumbled into one of our operations, they were made to lay off. It was for their benefit as well as MI5's or '6's operation. Policemen could get themselves hurt by crossing some of the people we dealt with.

"Did your boss say who?" I already knew he would not be told. Orders would have come direct from the Home Office.

"Only that the order came from high."

I thought over what he was saying. "So what do you want me to do?" I was not trying to be unkind, but considering how he had treated me, I was not in the mood to be friendly.

"I need that client list Carla. You're the only one I trust in that place."

I was taken aback by his words. He had never shown the least bit of trust towards me. In fact the only response he had shown me was hostile degradation. "You're just buttering me up. Don't think me to be such a fool." I spat the words at him, frustration building up inside at what I felt about him, and his ham fisted attempt to schmooze me. "You treat me with disrespect and then ask me for a favour like that?" I picked up his coat from the sofa and threw it at him. "I think you should leave."

Nick looked at the coat, then stood up. He didn't attempt to put it on. "I'm sorry, I have been cold towards you Carla. It's not what it seems." His eyes searched mine.

For the first time I saw a vulnerability about him I had not seen before. But I was angry, no, I was more than angry, I was seething. "So if it's not what it seems, what is it?" I stood in front of him and crossed my arms waiting for an explanation.

He placed the coat back on the sofa, but didn't take his eyes off me. "I just didn't expect to be attracted to you in the way I do." He looked uncomfortable. "I like you Carla. I like you a lot. And I just don't mean the way you look. There's something more to you. I can't believe I'm saying this."

I was dumbstruck. I couldn't believe he was saying it either. But as I looked at him, I knew he was telling the truth. I'd been trained by the best to see through liars and their lies. This guy was legit.

"I just can't get my head around what you do. Every time I think of you being with one of those clients, I feel sick, and I hate the way it makes me feel."

Amen, there brother. I knew just where he was coming from. Didn't I feel the same way? I hated the way I felt about Connie's choice of work. With guys like Sir Felix the thought sickened me to the stomach

I was still not going to let him off the hook. I'd had to endure his taunts and derision for too long. I pressed my fingers together. "Oh, and that's supposed to make everything OK is it? Just say sorry when you need something." I turned my back on him and began moving towards the door. I felt his hand on my shoulder.

I turned around as he edged towards me, his head bowed down above my face as his hand caressed my hair. I pushed him away, but he didn't let go. I could feel his breath on me as his mouth came down on mine. My body went into spasms as his lips brushed mine, his hands fingering through the lengths of my hair. I let his tongue probe the inside of my mouth, surprising myself, I was reciprocating as I met his tongue with my own. He held me close, close enough to feel his cock hard against me. God, how I wanted him.

I reached my hand to his face and pulled back. I could see the sadness in his eyes as I moved further away. We stood in silence. For the first time I thought I knew him. Resistance now was futile – I had none. I realised I had been waiting for this moment. I moved closer to him reaching up to his lips again as we locked our mouths to each other.

Feeling his hands reach every inch of my body, I felt on fire. Our kissing becoming urgent then almost frantic. His fingers found my breasts, and I shivered with pleasure as I felt his touch on them. I could feel my nipples erect under his fingers and without realising what was happening, I was helping him tug my top up over my head. I stood in front of him as I unhitched my bra and let it fall away from me. He leaned down in front of me, his tongue licking my nipples as his mouth swallowed my breast. I was almost coming already. I could feel the dampness spread between my legs.

I tugged his shirt off and undid his belt. He was too quick for me. Before I had time to feel his cock, his fingers had found the zip on my pants and he tugged them down, as he did so I stood out of them. He pulled my panties aside and put his mouth on my pussy. I yelped in delight as his tongue found the damp folds between my thighs, licking at my clit and plunging into me. I was close to coming, I had to pull away.

I pushed him onto the sofa and took his pants and boxers down. I gasped when I saw his cock. It was beautiful, thick and long. I cupped his balls in my hand as I went down on him, my mouth enclosing his head and shaft. He tasted beautiful as I drank up his pre-cum that was dripping from his cock. I could hear him gasp as I kept up the pressure with my tongue and hands. He pushed me away, breathing hard. Laying me on the floor, his fingers found my pussy again and I trembled under them. He was on top of me. I could see his cock coming towards me. And then I felt him. He was inside me. My god he felt so good. I clasped his cock deep inside me as I felt him invade every inch I had to offer. His mouth found mine and as he rhythmically fucked me, our tongues found each other. Harder he went, until I felt my body spasm and shudder as wave after wave of pleasure hit me. I had never had an orgasm like that before and could only watch as Nick collapsed onto me, sweat pouring from him.

I lay on the rug next to him, his arm around me. We were both spent. After a minute he leaned on his elbow and looked down on me. "My God, Carla, you're so beautiful." He kissed me again. I could feel the warmth of his skin as we lay in others arms. I wanted time to stand still, I didn't want the moment to end ever.

I watched the sun move across the window and sighed.

"What's the matter," Nick asked, looking at me?

"We can't lie like this all day can we? Wish we could though."

He smiled, and I knew there and then I loved him. Me Chastity Black in love. I never thought it could happen.

"Why can't we?"

"For one thing, we both have jobs to do." Before I had even finished the last word, I regretted it.

Nick looked at me, a shadow crossing his face, his brow wrinkled. "What do you mean jobs? You can't work for E after this?" He looked at me wounded, as though I had just plunged a knife into him.

I didn't know what to say. God, I wanted to tell him the truth, but if I did, what would it mean? He would blow my cover for one, and there was too much at stake. By tonight, if things went right, it would all be over, one way or another. I could not risk it, and I couldn't risk Nick getting involved or killed. These were the worst type of people we were dealing with. They wouldn't think anything about killing a copper.

"It's not what you think Nick. Look, I only have to do one thing tonight, and that's it, I'm out of E. You just need to trust me."

It was too late, he was up and dressing immediately. "I must have been mad to let this happen. I should have known that someone like you would be nothing more than a whore deep down."

I wrapped the throw from the sofa around me. For the first time ever, I felt ashamed of my nakedness. "Please Nick, call me tomorrow, I'll explain everything if I can."

He fished into his coat pocket and pulled out his wallet. Taking a bunch of twenty pound notes he flung them at my feet. "If I owe you any more, just send me a bill. I won't be contacting you again."

I stood there as I heard the front door slam behind him. I felt the tears pool in my eyes. He was gone.

Chapter Seventeen

I tried to drown the empty feeling I had. I doubt even if I told Nick the truth about my involvement with E, he would want anything to do with me. I had not trusted him enough. But how could I have with so much on the line?

I looked out of the window. The street was quiet. My body had calmed down. It had been such a long time since I had made love, if I had ever made love that is. Compared to the lovemaking with Nick, everything else seemed like just sex. There is a huge difference between the two. Until now I would never have believed it. It wasn't just the sexual desire, there was something else. Something I felt, like forgetting everything, even myself and melting into the other person. I sighed, realizing I had blown it with the only man I had felt something for.

I was brought back to the reality when my mobile sprung to life. It sounded hollow and far away as I picked it up.

"Hi, it's me. How did you get on?" Carl sounded serious. Of course he always sounded serious, but this time he spoke with a little more urgency.

"It's all set. I arrive on Fakhir's yacht tonight. I still have no plan, though." I switched the phone to the other hand and made my way into the kitchen. I opened the fridge and took the milk out. "Do you have any ideas?" I rested the milk on the counter and wrestled the flap up with my free hand swigging from the carton. Connie used to hate it when I did that when we were younger, it would drive her mad. A memory formed as I heard Carl talking on the other end of the line.

"I've managed to put a tap on Cordelia's phone in her office. She's due back in a bit, as soon as I get a chance I'll rig her mobile. Every call, text or email will go through us. Whatever she's planning, we'll know. We've got a detail on her. She can't cough without us knowing."

"What about Callaghan," I asked?

"Everyone's on high alert. I'll organise one of our guys to pick you up in a cab and drop you off. The Navy and the Coastguard will be close by in case the yacht is taken out to sea. Both our agencies will be standing by watching and ready. Even the CIA has offered us manpower. Everyone wants to see this Callaghan brought to heel. The world will be safer without him."

"And me?"

"You just concentrate on your end. Find where the KD-5 is being held. Knowing who the buyer is and where Callaghan plans to make the drop will be great, but locating the toxin is the number one priority. We can't afford it getting into the wrong hands."

"How are we going to communicate?"

"I'll be round within the next couple of hours if Bainbridge gets back in time. I'll rig you with some kit. It's all state of the art, so you'll have eyes and ears with you all the time."

"I'll have to be on my best behaviour then." I wasn't going to be getting undressed for the Prince this time. The boys at MI5 and '6' would love that. I'd never be able to live it down. That is if I survived the night. The thought struck me - these were serious criminals. If I messed up, there would be no second chance.

I still had some time to kill, and I felt less comfortable being left alone with my feelings about Nick than taking out a terrorist cell. I fingered the phone in my hand, hitting the speed dial.

"Hugo, it's Chastity."

"I was just about to call you too. I just had a meeting with MI6 and our boss at '5'. Looks like your involvement in this is now well in the open. As yet my complicit role in all this has not been uncovered."

"Shit. I'm so sorry. I won't land you in it, you know that? How much trouble am I in Hugo?"

"It could be worse. Just as well, they need you right now. As you know, things have taken a dramatic turn."

"The Pandora toxin?"

Hugo released a heavy breath on the other end of the line. "Yes, well that will do it. Thwarting a sale to a known terrorist group outranks employee misbehaviour every time. There will be reprimands, but not until we have the KD-5 in our protection. It's not only the Country that depends on you getting this right tonight. If it goes well your job may well depend on it too - that is if you have one after this. Sorry, Chas, it's unfair, but you knew the risks when you started out on this."

So even if I find the KD-5, take Callaghan and Bainbridge in, I'm out of a job. Perfect. "That's OK Hugo, you're right, I did know what the consequences would be. But I had to do it for Connie."

"I know Chastity. I'll put a word in for you. If it does go well tonight and we locate the toxin, I'm sure they will look on your off site investigation with a little more leniency."

I hoped so. "Listen, Hugo, there's something else I wanted to ask you."

I could hear Hugo exhale - I was testing his patience. "Go on," he said?

"Whatever happens tonight, make sure that Callaghan and Bainbridge are brought to justice. After everything that's happened, I don't want anyone to forget Connie and Dana Bryce."

Hugo went silent on the line. "Yes Chastity," he finally replied. "I promise."

I said goodbye, hanging up while I moved towards the window. Pushing the blind to one side, I looked at the street below. I don't know why, but I hoped to see Nick there, maybe parked up in his car. But no, the street was all too quiet.

It took me no time at all to get showered and ready. My hair took the most time teasing it into elaborate curls. By the time Carl arrived, I was dressed in a long classy black satin number and looked like I was worth every penny of E's £10,000 fee.

"Wow. Got to say Chastity," began Carl as he looked me up and down when I swung open my apartment door, "you look amazing."

I smiled. Yeah, sure I scrubbed up well when the occasion called for it. "Is everything set?" As I let him in I noticed the briefcase he was holding. "That the kit," I asked?

Carl nodded. "Everything is here. We'll have eyes and ears on you. I just need to fit it."

I watched as he took out a small plastic earplug that fitted snugly into my inside ear. It was discreet enough from even the most prying eyes. Next he pinned a small brooch to my dress. It was an exquisite swirling design embedded with diamonds.

"This is your mic. It's fitted with the latest nano-type technology. We'll be able to hear everything that goes on around you." Taking a necklace from the folds of his pocket, he blew on it to remove any dust. It didn't look anything special, just a gold pendant with a black onyx. "This is our eyes. Like the brooch," said Carl, it's Nano tech, and has the smallest lens on the market. We'll get to see what's happening. Just remember we'll be watching, so any little trips to the Ladies-be aware."

I understood what he meant. It also meant there could be no undressing or sexual antics with the Prince while I was wearing this kit. I didn't want to see the smirks from my colleagues next time I had to pass by them in Thames House - that was if I had a job left after this.

I checked one last time in the mirror, then picked up a black pashima, wrapping it around my shoulders. It was showtime.

Just as Carl said, the black cab outside had one of our men at the wheel. He nodded as I got in the back. Carl smiled. "Remember, we're watching you all the time. First priority is to locate the canister. If you can find where the meet is and who the buyer is, all the better. But it will mean nothing if we don't get our hands on the toxin."

"I know all too well what needs to be done Carl." I looked at him as he closed the cab door and we drove off. I watched him through the back window become a speck on the pavement as we got further until he was no longer in sight. Focussing on my breathing, I gathered myself for the task in hand. I was starting to doubt my abilities. *Could I pull this off?*

By the time we reached the dockside, it had grown dark. '6's agent let me out of the cab saying nothing. I knew the protocol - everything had to look cosha. I held my purse in my hand. It held nothing but a lipstick and my keys, and of course my mobile phone. At least if everything in there was scrutinized it would pass any inspection. My lipstick had been hollowed out at the flank. It allowed me to fill it with enough pills to knock out a horse if need be. And judging by the Prince's libido, I'd need them all.

As I walked up towards Fakhir's yacht, I was met by Callaghan at the end of the walkway. With a narrowing of his eyes, he let me past. He did not look happy to see me. I could feel his eyes bore into my back as I climbed the red carpet that adorned the planked avenue to the Prince's yacht.

"He's waiting for you down below." The words were flung at me as an insinuation rather than a greeting. Once on board, he followed me down the steps. I knew the way. I felt insecure and vulnerable, having Callaghan to my back. His height and size dwarfed me. I was relieved to see the Prince waiting for me just outside his suite.

"My dear Mercedes. How wonderful it is to see you again, and how beautiful and elegant you look tonight." He stretched out his hand, guiding me into his quarters. I flashed a quick glance behind me, Callaghan was still there. He looked at me then gave the briefest of nods to Fakhir before striding off back towards the steps.

The Prince looked cool in his linens. His dark skin a warm contrast to the crisp white clothing he was wearing. "A drink," he asked?

I moved towards him, taking the Cristal from the bucket. "Let me my Prince. I want tonight to be special for you. I will be your willing servant this evening. Your wish will be my desire." I was cringing. God knows what the team listening was thinking. According to Carl, even the Home Secretary was listening in on tonight's operation.

"If that is what you want Mercedes, then who am I to argue with such a beautiful woman." He turned and sat on the massive bed, his eyes never leaving my body.

"Why don't you put some music on?" I needed to divert his gaze while I laced his drink with the pills, giving them time to dissolve.

"He reached for a remote control. The music came on, exotic and sultry. It reminded me of the nights in Morocco. "Is this OK," he asked?

"Yes," I replied as I turned and smiled. "Perfect." I watched the little white pills melt into the bubbles of the champagne.

"Here," I said, passing him the flute of Cristal.

"Thank you. I have been dreaming of tasting your beautiful pussy again and licking your breasts. I was so upset that we did not finish our business the other night."

I got a sudden bout of stage fright. Aware that there were ears listening to this conversation, I hoped the drug would kick in soon and knock him out. I forced a smile.

"Now, come here Mercedes. I wish to see you naked again. Undress for me." It was not a question, but a demand.

Damn, this was going to be trickier than I thought. I went over to him, ignoring his request. Instead, I sat next to him and looked into his eyes whilst fingering the fabric of his tunic. "This is nice Champaign."

I watched as he swilled back the last of his glass. I only hoped the drug worked soon. His hand found the zip at the side of my dress and was sliding it down as his lips kissed my neck. I was starting to feel a little panicky. I sat back a little and looked at him. His eyes had become glassy and I could see him sway.

"I'm sorry Mercedes, I do not feel too well." The words trailed off as he fell backwards onto the bed. Thank God, I thought. He was asleep.

"Great Chastity, now it's time to get moving." I could hear Carl's voice in my ear. The piece he had fitted me with was clear. This was his show, he was in charge. I just hoped he knew what he was doing.

"Check the hold. It can be the only place Callaghan could store the Pandora vial. As soon as we have visual, we get our guys in and you out. OK?"

"Got it," I replied. I opened the door to the hallway and peered both ways. It was clear. From memory, I knew the steps to the hold had to be to my right - I'd have remembered if I'd have seen any on the way to the Prince's quarters.

I could hear disembodied voices floating down from above. So far - so good, I thought. I slipped off my Blahnik's and edged my way down the corridor. It was times like these I wished I had a firearm at my disposal. I could not take the chance, if I was searched, I would have had to explain to Callaghan why a high class escort carried a gun. The only protection an escort would have came in a wrapper and would be made of rubber.

I spotted the carpeted steps going below. Being careful to remain silent, I tiptoed down. The light was diffused here, not as bright as the main living quarters. The steps rounded near the bottom and I was hit with the aroma of food and good coffee. As I saw the light, I knew I had reached the kitchen. I could hear voices and was reminded of the urgency by Carl in my ear.

Just before I reached the kitchen, set back just to the left was a metal door. Its sign told me it was for staff only. There was a metal bar across it, the same as fire doors. Pushing it with my weight, it swung open making a whining metallic din. I flinched hoping it was not heard by the kitchen staff.

Emergency lighting sprang into life as I entered the depths of the hold. As my eyes became adjusted to the gloom, I descended a set of metal steps. I could see a number of crates and boxes nestled within the room. Food and supplies by the look of it. "I'm inside," I whispered, hoping Carl could pick up my transmission. "Are you there?" There was no reply. For all the technical advancements the secret service had at their disposal, they were yet to find a two way radio communication that worked in dead-zones. Fat lot of good this kit was doing for me down here in the depths. I was alone in this now.

I edged my way around the hold. It was larger than I expected, but then again, it was quite a yacht. It seemed more like a liner than a boat. As I got further into the room, I could see some old boxes at the back. They looked buried under what looked like tarpaulin or thick green, plastic sheeting.

As I pulled back the covering, I realised I had found Callaghan's stash. They were metal rectangular crates about six feet in length and two feet in diameter. I shuddered as a thought crossed my mind. They looked more like metal coffins than containers.

I looked at the padlocks, then taking the sliver of metal from my hair, I picked at the locks one by one until the padlocks sprang open. Pushing the lid up, I saw the guns and comms kits inside each of the containers. Weapons from Russia, the US and a number of grenades, enough to blow a small town up.

I wasn't sure what I was looking for. All I knew was that the KD-5 would be kept in an airtight container. Perhaps this was where the Prince's security kept their firearms for emergencies? Then I saw it. At the opposite end of one of the crates, was a large aluminium case. With considerable care I pulled it free from its sheer fabric dust cover and lifted it out. With no lock, I opened it. Inside was what I was looking for - the KD-5. It was only a cylinder, and looked harmless enough, but I knew there was enough here to kill most of London. I twisted the container, and pulled up the metal latch. The vial of pink liquid was secure. It was inside reinforced sheet glass. It was only as much as a beaker full. I found it unbelievable that such a small amount could wipe out cities. I replaced the vial back in its metal container. Remembering the security protocol - it had to stay at a stable temperature. If one of those grenades blew, the heat would activate the toxin.

I still couldn't get Carl - the line was still dead. I had a choice. I could take the case and try to make it off the yacht, or leave it and get up top and make contact with Carl and send the message to deploy the men. I was loathe to leave it there in the hold. I was about to turn when I noticed the light had dimmed a little. I was too late, the light had not weakened by accident, it was a shadow cast by a figure. Just before I saw the fist coming at me, I saw Callaghan's hulking frame loom over me.

Chapter Eighteen

The first thing I felt when I came to was the plastic tie digging into the flesh of my wrist. My hands were bound behind my back. Through a haze, I opened my eyes. It took me a moment to realise - Callaghan had surprised me. I struggled against the bind, but all I succeeded in doing was rip into my skin more, I winced at the pain.

It was dark, my head was throbbing and tender. The only sound I could hear was my own breathing. And I was cold. I shivered. I only hoped that Carl had everything under control. Without radio contact, how was I going to alert him? Their immediate presence was to be on my call. Only when the KD-5 was located where they to engage and capture. I prayed they would arrive before Callaghan came back.

That was a point, where had he gone? I sat there struggling a little longer in my ties before I heard the whine of the metal door and a sliver of light illuminating the darkness within the room.

"Ah, you're awake I see."

The diffused lighting came on overhead, their stripped beams, making me blink. Callaghan stood above me. He looked as though he was concentrating on a puzzle. He stooped down in front of me on his haunches, his face only millimetres away from mine. I could feel his breath on me.

"So who are you?"

His cruel eyes searched mine.

"I don't know what you mean, "I lied. "You know who I am. I'm here on a date."

The hand came out fast slapping my face. The force sent my head reeling to the side. I could taste the coppery bitterness of blood in my mouth. Bastard.

"Don't lie to me," he said. His eyes flashed. This man was used to hurting people. I knew the look well. "Has that bitch sent you to keep an eye on me?"

I could only assume he meant Bainbridge. I knew I was going to get another smack, but too much was at stake, "I told you I don't know what you mean."

I stiffened while I waited for him to strike me again, but instead he just continued searching my face. He was still stooping in front of me, his eyes drilling into me as though he could just retrieve what he wanted to know from staring at me.

"Look," I said, "I was just looking for the kitchen. The Prince sent me for more Champagne. Now if this is not part of some kinky fantasy, I insist you untie me and let me go."

The smile that spread across his face disarmed me - I wasn't expecting it.

"Let's try again shall we," Callaghan said? "The Prince is out of it, no doubt drugged. The alarm on this door is triggered in the security suite when it is opened. Now we both know why you're here. What I don't know is who sent you and what you're up to."

I saw the flash of steel in his hand. I knew what it was.

"You see this knife," he said, holding it up a few centimeters from my face, "has caused more pain than you could imagine. And if you don't tell me what I want to know, you are going to find out for yourself." He held the knife to my cheek. I could feel the cold steel on my skin.

"It would be such a pity to ruin a face as beautiful as yours. Mind you, by the time I'm finished, you won't be needing it at the bottom of the river."

I looked around the room, unsure of what I was going to do.

"No use in screaming down here, darling, no one will hear you."

As he moved closer with the knife I tried to scrabble backwards on the cold floor using my bare heels. It was like treading in treacle - I was going nowhere. I was about to butt him in the head when I felt him slump on top of me. It took me a second before it registered. Nick stood behind him holding a fire extinguisher in his hand. He'd knocked Callaghan out.

"What the...?"

Nick smiled. "You can tell me what the hell is going on in a minute, but right now, we need to get you untied and out of here." He took the knife that Callaghan had held and cut through the plastic ties.

I threw my arms around him. I had never been so happy to see someone in all my life. "How did you know I was here," I asked?

"I'm a cop, I followed you of course. I wasn't going to let the woman I love get away from me so easily. I needed to know what you were about."

I only heard the bit where he told me he loved me - I couldn't believe what he was saying. He held me in his arms for a moment and released a long sigh. He dropped the knife onto the floor where it landed with a metallic clank.

"So when I got here, I knew something was going on. I spotted the men in the unmarked cars around the site. I can spot spook activity a mile away. It all tied in Carla - me getting told to stand down on the case and leave well alone. It had to be MI5 or '6'."

"It was both," I said, unable to hide my smile. "And my name is Chastity, not Carla. Connie was my sister." I saw the relief in his face as he took my hand, but as I watched something in his face changed. A look of surprise washed over him as he fell forward and I saw the blood.

It was only when I saw Callaghan standing behind the slumped body of Nick that I knew.

Callaghan still had the bloody knife in his hand. I didn't think, I was on my feet in an instant. I circled him as he held the knife out in front. I wanted to see Nick. His soft moaning told me he was still alive, but I did not know how hurt he was. He needed emergency attention.

"Who would have thought a little tart like you would get in the way?" Callaghan lunged the knife towards me making me take a step backwards.

"Life is full of surprises," I replied through gritted teeth. This was a trained military killer. I watched as the glint of silver in his hand remained steady.

As he sprung forward, I kicked my leg out, knocking the knife from his hand. I had only a brief glimpse as the shock registered on his face. Moving in fast I hit him hard with the heel of my hand into his nose, while bringing the side of my foot down on his knee with all the force I had. He went down, his eyes streaming. I punched him hard in the jaw for good measure and felt the pain rocket through my wrist as my fist hit bone, sending a jolt up my arm. I'd most likely broken my hand, but it was worth it. Callaghan went down, the knife falling from him.

I kicked the blade away from him with my foot. It was already too late; he was pulling a Glock from under his jacket. I recognised the gun immediately. It was a precision made firearm. From this distance, if he aimed and shot I'd be dead.

I ducked to the left, landing on the floor, scraping my knees on the metal grid beneath me. Lifting the gun, he pointed it at me. For a moment the gunshot deafened me. I watched as the bullet hit an overhead pipe. Before Callaghan had the chance to recover and shoot, I jumped on him, kicking him in the groin. He let out a cry before I punched him again in the face, this time he stayed down. He was unconscious.

I ran to Nick. He was lying in a pool of his own blood. His waxen skin was covered in cold sweat. He was losing consciousness.

"Are you OK," he mumbled between shallow breaths?

I held his head in my arms. "Hey, I'm fine. You just hold on while I get some help. Callaghan will be out for a while."

I found some electrical cord in a box, and tied up Callaghan with the flex. He wasn't going anywhere, but I wanted to be careful all the same. I sniffed. There was a strange smell filling the space. I knew it well - gas. Callaghan must have shot the pipe that led from the gas tanks. I looked along the overhead piping. It fed the kitchen.

Aware that the Pandora toxin was an immediate threat, I looked at Nick. Could I leave him? If the KD-5 got above 300 degrees, the whole of London would be affected. Thousands would be killed. It was him or the toxin, an impossible choice. I ran to the kitchen shouting.

Surprised by a girl dressed in long black satin screaming at them to turn off the hobs, the kitchen staff gawped at me slack-jawed. With their Philippine appearance, I didn't think they could understand a thing I was saying. They stood staring at me and then to one another.

It was too late. I heard a whoosh, the kitchen was about to blow. I ducked behind the metal door while the room exploded, sending metal and glass at every corner. Breathing heavy, I waited until all I could hear was the fire envelope the room. I had to get to the toxin and Nick before the whole yacht blew.

None of the kitchen staff could have survived the blast, but how many people were on board? I raced back to the hold. Nick was just about conscious. I took a chance. Taking the KD-5 from its crate, wrapping it in a nearby fire blanket, I held it to me as though it was a fragile baby.

I took one last look at Nick. *Please be OK*, I thought, as I ran from the hold.

Sprinting up to the deck I was met by Carl and his team, including a troop of snipers in bio-suits. The blast had caused them to storm the boat. "Quick," I shouted to them. "I need a medic now. I've got a detective down there bleeding out." I only hoped the blade had missed his kidneys and liver. "The yacht's going to blow."

"OK Chas," replied Carl. "Have you located the poison?"

"Here," I answered. I passed him the swaddled fire blanket. "Be careful." I ran back to the hold, hoping Nick was still alive. He was, but I was not sure for how long.

I stood stunned as my colleagues and the medics went about their jobs. I didn't care about the KD-5, the smell of Gas that still hung in the air or Callaghan. I followed them as they dragged both Nick and Callaghan onto the dockside away from the immediate danger of an explosion.

I could hardly breathe for worry as I watched the medics stem Nick's bleeding and put a line in him. I waited to find out if he would make it, and only hoped he would be OK. Somehow, I had fallen in love with Nick. It was only at the thought of losing him did it hit me hard. This was the man. I had never wanted or cared for any man the way I did for Nick. Admitting the truth to myself was both a relief and now a massive fear. To find out you love someone at the same moment they could die, was not something my training had prepared me for.

I looked at the medics, waiting.

One of them turned to me, concern etched on his face. "We've stabilised him for now, but we need to get him to hospital, the sooner the better."

It was the best I could hope for under the circumstances.

I turned and saw Carl looking at me. "We got the KD-5 Chastity just in time, but it was bloody close. I'm sorry about Nick. Is he going to be OK?"

I shrugged my shoulders.

Carl lowered his head. "Looks like we got your sister's killer."

It was a small compensation. I was losing too much. "Not quite," I replied. "There's still another person responsible sitting out there."

"Bainbridge?"

I nodded. "She's just as much the murderer as Callaghan. She set up my sister, not to mention Dana Bryce."

"We'll get her picked up," said Carl about to call in the order through his fitted mic.

"No," I said planting my hand on his arm. "I'll do this. I've waited a long time to get those responsible for Connie's murder."

Carl looked dubious. I could see he was thinking it over. I knew what was going on in his head.

"I won't hurt her unless she attacks me first. Trust me."

"OK. But you're not going alone." He spoke into his mouthpiece and asked that I be accompanied to E's headquarters for the arrest of Cordelia Bainbridge. With reluctance Carl passed me his gun and ordered one of his men to find me some boots and fit me with a Kevlar vest.

The place was silent when we got there. The gate was wide open and the house too quiet. There were no security personnel and Childers was not at her usual spot behind the reception desk in the foyer. I had three details with me - all men. Carl had insisted that the three MI6 agents go with me, not so much for my own protection but for Bainbridge's.

He wasn't daft; he knew I was likely to kill her if I got the chance. MI5 and '6' still needed to know who the buyer was. Sometimes the threats to this Country can come from many strange places.

The three agents nodded to me as one stayed on the ground floor, while the other two went below to the security room. When they came back they shrugged. The place was deserted. While the three men scouted around, I walked along the corridor to Cordelia's office. It was shut, but unlocked. I swung the door open, my firearm held loose in my right hand. She was slumped forward on her desk - her head lying in blood. I checked behind the office door. Callaghan could not have killed Bainbridge; he was at the boat all the time. I moved closer to Cordelia's body and lifted her head.

Her throat had been cut. By the looks of it someone had come up behind her and held her head while they sliced her.

I usually join the dots quite fast, but something was eating at me. If someone was to come up on her, she would have had to be familiar with them; otherwise she would not have remained seated. As I absorbed this information, the creaking wood of the door alerted me.

Childers stood in front of me. She was wearing the same woolen skirt and purple tights. She looked at me. Her eyes moved from Bainbridge to me. At first I didn't understand. It took me a little time before I recognised Childers expression - It was one of disappointment. She sighed, her shoulders sagging.

"It was you," I said? All the time I thought it was Bainbridge, but it was Childers. I could not believe it. This mousy middle aged woman was responsible for the attempt on the most devastating threat this Country had ever seen.

"Surprised?" With wide eyes, she stood rooted to the spot. Tugging at her fingers, she looked at me.

I didn't need to answer; my face must have said it all. I looked again at Bainbridge.

"It's such a pity you had to find out. I should have known you were up to something. My client won't take kindly to losing his product." She sounded like a child trying to explain her bad behaviour to a parent.

"If you mean the KD-5, then he'll just have to live with it." I pointed the gun at her. "Do you know what that stuff does? It would have killed thousands of people?"

Childers shrugged. There seemed something broken about her. She looked more like a petulant child who had her toy taken off her than an arms dealer. What had happened to this woman to make her this way?

"Of course I know what it does. Oh come on, if I didn't take it someone else would have sooner or later. Besides, don't you think our own Government had not thought of selling it?"

"That's not the point," I replied. "How on earth did you steal it? I mean someone like you --"

"That's the point. Someone like me indeed. I had worked at Porton Down for fifteen years. Day after day doing their admin, the yes sir, the no sir. I may as well have not existed." She tugged at her fingers, her mouth trembling. "Someone like me becomes invisible; someone like me gets overlooked and laughed at. So someone like me wanted to turn those tables. They won't be laughing at me anymore, that's for certain."

"That's why you did it? You stole the worst biological weapon known to man because you were pissed off?" I still couldn't believe it.

Childers slumped into the brown leather chair by the door. She looked defeated. I could see by the wrinkles and dark circles around her spectacle clad eyes that she was worn out.

"Years of my life I had given my Country, and why," she murmured? "So that I could get laughed at and cast aside? They were going to lay me off. After all I'd given them. And what for? I had no husband, no children, and no family. I gave up on all possibility of a normal life - and I did it all for my Country. All so I could have a career and do their damn paperwork, do their research, amend databases and fetch them coffee. All the office drudgery you could imagine." Childers looked beyond me, at the window at the far end of the room. "I still had the passcodes, the point of entry and admission to the laboratories on site."

"You killed my sister, you bitch."

"The journalist?" She looked puzzled.

"No, Connie. She was my little sister and you had her killed. Was it you or Callaghan, who murdered her?"

Childers raised her eyebrows. "Yes, I can see the similarity between you now. I wondered who you reminded me of." She looked at me, bending her head to one side. "No, that was Callaghan. Your sister found out about the deal and had to be dealt with. It was such a shame. She overheard me, you see, with our friend Callaghan. I liked your sister, but what could I do? She put two and two together. Callaghan was a pig for what he did to your sister. I didn't want him to hurt her the way he did. He was just supposed to shoot her and dispose of her." Childers tugged at her fingers with more urgency. "The Bryce woman was snooping and somehow your sister passed what she knew about us onto her. But what does it matter now?"

I couldn't believe how matter of fact she sounded. It was like she was explaining a recipe for cake rather than a murder.

"Why kill Cordelia?" I glanced at Bainbridge's body.

"Because she got too close, she found out who I was."

"You mean she realized you were a terrorist?" I snorted and shook my head. It all made sense, as mad as it seemed. Callaghan had started work for Fakhir around the same time Childers started working at E.

"No, not exactly," she said. "She went digging, looking for the owner of E."

"The owner?" I was confused. I had always thought Cordelia was the owner.

"I established E before I left the civil service. I made it look like it was owned by a consortium. I had myself hired here and arranged for Bainbridge to be in charge. She never met the owner and was under strict orders not to go looking. But she just had to go snooping, didn't she?"

I raised my arms "How the hell could you have afforded this place on a civil service wage?"

"At Porton Down I was responsible for the admin on budgets, operations and finance. Do you have any idea how much budget that place is given? It was easy to siphon amounts off here and there for non-existent laboratory research."

She stood, glancing downwards, looking pathetic as she stood in silence. She reminded me of a naughty school kid caught cheating on a test. I held the gun out in front of me. "You're coming with me."

Childers stood up. I saw the other three agents behind her, their weapons in their hands should they need it. I nodded to them.

There was something missing from her grey eyes. The lights seemed on, but no one was at home. I motioned to one of the agent's to cuff her. Childers turned, looking behind her. Her eyes widened as the light finally switched on inside her head.

"No," she said. "I can't go with you. They'll kill me - I'll be dead by morning."

I didn't understand what she meant. I remembered the hooded men that ransacked Dana Bryce's apartment. One had to be Callaghan, but who was the other?

Before I had the chance to ask her, she slipped her hand inside the oversized pocket of her long grey cardigan. She was pulling something bulky from it.

I could hear myself shout out to her, as it dawned on me what she was doing. It all happened so fast. I shouted at the agents to stand down, but it was too late, the tall guy had his gun out and I heard the shot ring out as though watching it from outside my body. They thought Childers was pulling a gun.

I bent down to her and saw what she was holding in her hand - a mobile phone.

"I thought it was a gun. I had to fire." The agent shrugged his shoulders.

"I know," I replied. And I did know. Childers knew exactly what she was doing. She was scared of someone else that was for sure. Perhaps the buyer or someone she was working with or for. She knew the agent would shoot the minute she went into her pocket. It was what she wanted.

I knew I would never get those answers I needed from Childers now - she was dead and her secrets along with her.

Epilogue

I stood over the grave and watched as they lowered the casket. The wind slapped at my face. The loss was unbearable. I felt Hugo's arm wrap around my shoulder. What was it Shakespeare said about love and loss?

I could not help the tears from letting loose. On that grey day I cried. I didn't want to think about what would happen next. I just wanted the day to end.

Hugo guided me back to the car. "S have exonerated you. At least you still have a job Chastity." He grabbed my hand, giving it a gentle squeeze. It was cold comfort and little compensation for what I had lost. But at least it was over, and Hugo had been wonderful over the last few days, he was my rock throughout the pain that followed. I was left alone to grieve. I smiled at him. It was bittersweet, but under the circumstances, it was the best I could muster.

"Why don't you stay with me Chastity, at least for a few days?"

"Thanks Hugo, I appreciate it, but I'm OK, really. I have something I need to do first before I go home."

Hugo nodded. He understood.

I got into my Audi. After giving him a brief wave, I slithered in beside the wheel and pulled out onto the road, making my way past the centre of town. The car park was near to full when I entered the hospital, but I managed to secure what looked like the last spot.

I never liked hospitals. They reminded me of death. I sniffed at the antiseptic and pushed the elevator button.

I had to keep it together, lest more tears threaten the day. The ward was quiet and bereft of any personality. Its stark, sterile smell greeted me as I walked to the last room and to the bed at the window.

"You're looking better," I said.

He was looking out beyond the hospital grounds as though his mind was somewhere else. He turned when he heard my voice and smiled up at me. "You OK," Nick asked?

"Yeah. It was dignified. I said my goodbyes to Connie. It's just that as I watched the casket, it all came back. The childhood things, if you know what I mean?"

"Yes Chastity, I know." His solemn eyes didn't flicker.

I leaned over and kissed him on the lips. I was careful not to press into him. He was still sore from the surgery. He was lucky; the knife had missed his liver by a hair's breadth. I still got the tingling and the shivers each time I touched him, no matter how brief.

"Did they find out who Callaghan and Childers were selling the toxin to?"

I shook my head. It had been five days since the raid on the yacht.

"Callaghan was immediately whisked away. I believe the CIA has him now and they are not as hospitable as us Brits. I've got it on good authority that he will suffer for what he has done. But it was Childers who brought in the buyer and brokered the deal. Callaghan knows nothing."

"Where are they keeping him - Guantanamo Bay?"

I nodded. "Callaghan will be locked up for the rest of his life, however long that is. The Saudi Government however, has made a profitable deal with ours. It seems that we had saved them a lot of embarrassment by catching Callaghan. I doubt they would want to be implicated with a terrorist attack. And we did save a member of their Royal family."

The investigation that followed revealed Childers and Callaghan had found each other while she was monitoring him during an op involving a diplomat in Russia. Childers saw her chance and contacted Callaghan. "Everything was orchestrated Nick,"

I ran my fingers through his hair. I was more than grateful that he had lived - and to think I had actually hated him once. I bit into my lower lip as I recalled what Hugo had told me at the debriefing. "I was right about them using Prince Fakhir for his diplomatic status." I poured Nick a glass of water from the jug on the cabinet next to him. His eyes followed me. "Through it, they had been transporting arms around the world. I had to concede, I had got it wrong about Bainbridge - she was completely blameless. Her only crime was trying to protect the reputation of the agency."

Nick took the glass, sipping from it slowly. "It was a pity you didn't get their buyer's name or whoever it was that Childers was scared of."

I shrugged. He was right, but at least they didn't have the Pandora toxin. I shuddered at the thought of the damage it would have done had it been released.

After his surgery, I'd told Nick everything. OK, not everything, if you know what I mean? And if you don't mind, I'll be keeping my past escapades quiet if you please?

The End